PRAISE FOR *THESE BONES*

"Chenault's short but powerful gothic work blends the best elements of folklore, horror, the blues, and archival history in resonant and lyrical prose. Fans of alternate histories, suspenseful literary fiction, and Black speculative fiction will be hooked on piecing together this intricate, entrancing tale."

—*Publishers Weekly* (starred review)

"Kayla Chenault has created something truly exquisite: a rich tapestry whose gorgeous poetics never obscure its themes or narrative. From beginning to end, *These Bones* is a sheer pleasure of Dalloway-esque perspectives, post-modernist structures, joined histories, and the ghosts they reveal."

—Stacy D. Flood, author of *The Salt Fields*

"What a remarkable book. A generational history viewed obliquely through vignettes of various voices, songs, sermons, and ephemera full of magical realism, horror, righteous anger, sorrow, betrayal, love, and revenge. Utterly original. It's a gut punch."

—Alana Haley, Nicola's Books

"Chenault brings forth a history that isn't buried as far underground as once thought, a history soiled with horror and ferocity that finds harmony in the stunning prose."

—Caitlin Chung, author of *Ship of Fates*

THESE BONES

THESE BONES

BY KAYLA CHENAULT

LANTERNFISH PRESS

PHILADELPHIA

Lanternfish Press
399 Market Street, Suite 360
Philadelphia, PA 19106
lanternfishpress.com

Cover Design: Kimberly Glyder

"Abandoned Farm" by Tequask, CC BY-SA 4.0, via Wikimedia Commons
Liljenquist Family Collection of Civil War Photographs (Library of Congress)

Printed in the United States of America.
25 24 23 22 21   1 2 3 4 5

Library of Congress Control Number: 2020951741
Print ISBN: 978-1-941360-55-2
Digital ISBN: 978-1-941360-56-9

DEDICATION

To Janet, Jo, Jeff, Jack, Brent, Paul,
and of course Patrick Brettschneider,
and in memory of Richard Chenault II.

CAST OF CHARACTERS

I. THE BRAMBLE PATCH

The Lyons Family

Markum "King" Lyons
Ma Lyons
Dinah Lyons
Lazarus Lyons
Esther Lyons
Odessa Lyons
Wanhope Elizabeth "Bit" Lyons
The other Lyons children ("Them Others")

The Barghest's Girlie Show

The Barghest
Jessup
Ida
Winnifred
Fannie

Bertha's Kin

Bertha
Tempess
Auntie Rhea
Tata Duende
Selene, or "Moon-child"
Snow-baby

The Tellers

Grandma Ady
Mother
Bessie Teller-Chapman
Tommy "Bobwhite" Teller

II. NAPOLEONVILLE

The Kincaids

Rev. Jonah Kincaid
Eugenia Kincaid
Samuel Kincaid
Penelope "Sistie" Kincaid
Jacob Jonah "JJ" Kincaid
Croswell Kincaid

The Aileys

Dr. Peter Ailey
Verity Ailey
Geraldine "Deena" Ailey
Sally Ailey

The Keiths

Richard Keith
Dorotheé "Dolly" Keith
Marie-Anne Keith
Aimee Keith

Dear Dr. W. E. Lyons-Harris,

*I am writing you to deliver the enclosed photograph.
My name is Hannah Ickes, and I'm an undergrad student
in the archaeology program at Vanderbilt University.
This summer, I got the opportunity to work with the City
of Napoleonville Historical Society on the newest edition
of their local history book. We went to this site while we
were there. We think it was your childhood home, because
according to some records we found, the people who lived
in this house were the Lyons family, and from all the
further research we could do we found that you are the
only member of your family still alive.*

*I figured you'd be interested in seeing your old house.
I also wondered if you would mind answering a couple of
questions about your life growing up. First of all, the first
edition of the history guide said that the African-American*

side of town was called the Bramble Patch during your childhood. Could you give us some more information on that? What was it like being from the Bramble Patch? (Any anecdotes would be super helpful, thanks!) Also: you have this amazing life story about leaving Napoleonville and becoming a pediatric surgeon. I wonder how you were able to accomplish that, especially living in a time where the odds were stacked against you so much?

Please feel free to write me back at your earliest convenience. Thank you so much. I hope this photo brings you some joy, and I hope this note finds you well.

Sincerely,
Hannah Ickes

THESE BONES

Dear Miss Ickes,

My body is hobbled. De-threaded. As if every stitch and sinew and bone has been ripped away from the fabric that was once my body, and I am what is left. You're lucky that you wrote me when you did.

I am sentimental in my old age. In these latter days, away from the Bramble Patch, I am unsure if I can recall much of its lingua franca, but still I know the blessings and cusses and slurs very well. For example, I know that I'm colored. So, I know when I've been insulted.

All things hang upon the tempting banality of a decent life. I don't think you're looking for ghosts. No. You're just unearthing a starved beast.

Some people said that the Bramble Patch was built on the bones of its dead. The man I called "Daddy"— Markum "King" Lyons—that's what he told me often. I understand you academics are now looking for the evidence of that history. Well, King told me every house there had a foundation made of calcium and marrow, but I think he made it up to scare me. Trouble is, I'm not sure. So, if you can trace the lineage of a curse with your toolkit, I'd wager my soul against yours that the cornerstones of bones will ugly up your dreams for the dig site.

It was a kiln made from hymns, spirituals, and clapping games. And we were its golems, the not-quite-monsters.

I was buckskinned, like my mama, and by my mama I mean the woman who birthed me and died. Anyway, I was buckskinned and I had scabbed knees, and so the white folk decided they were going to stuff me for their trophy room. Like they did with my mama when they found her. But they got other people instead. I didn't know what a golem was, but I felt like one—made of clay. There was the Barghest. All of his world was built on top of other people's bones. Like the bones of Lazarus and Bessie and 'Livia and my mama, and others too.

When I was in medical school, I spent time looking at babies in jars—the never-born. Some still looked like seahorses in formaldehyde. Some were covered in fuzz. One specimen had two heads and two underdeveloped penises. They would have shared nothing but hunger and thirst, two lungs and one liver and a spleen. (Suppose: one had left the mother's faith of Catholicism and become agnostic but the other dreamt of becoming a priest; how could the first endure the other and vice versa?) These memories keep me up at night.

And the Barghest was more worrisome than that.

Sincerely,
Wanhope Lyons

IN THE SUMMER OF 1909

At the edge of New England, the world hung in place. The firmament frothed, salt eroded, and barnacles crusted, as all the old sailors and fishermen tried to find their land legs again. Everything was always gray. Gray eyes, hair and peacoats, parasols and sky, sea and people—especially, gray people. The people were barnacled, and the weather was constant. Only the sea could change.

At the whalers' end of the harbor, busk upon busk of marine skeleton was carved away from ivory blubber. The blubber tumbled and spilled and gurgled in the mud. Next, crimson would gush from the wound, splattering the harbor. Stray dogs would lap at the puddle of sanguine nourishment. With adipose and hemoglobin and dark gray dermis removed, only the stark bones remained.

Then came the quiet stitching of a seamstress, hunching vulture-like to weave the bones between strips of cotton. The harpy liked to curse each garment, laces and eyelets and all they held together. "Stays and bodies to break. Cinched waists under cuirass, collapsible lungs of broken wind." With bitter fingers she wove the curses into the corsets. Each curse ached her joints, creaking them, turning her nose beaklike and the hoods of her eyelids leaden, and she would hover over her work, stretch her wings, and screech her curses. Then the corsets made with malice were shipped off to stores, where they would end up in the hands of all manner of women, highborn and low. A corset is an equalizer for lady and whore.

Now the whalebone indents, raging red, marked Jess's bare torso. These rakings were the murdered odontoceti's last act of brutality. Jess tried to catch a fraction of her breath. She had danced for nickels, she had shimmied with zeal and hollered where the moment called for it, and made men forget their worries and wives. She should be much less winded than she was in that moment.

High yellow and modest as she was, burlesque never suited her, though it sustained her. Her hair fell in angelic ringlets, a cascade of them, in fact, and the scent of vanilla followed her, lovesick. Her suitors were many but her lovers were none.

In front of her stood the Barghest, that big-toothed, sharp-clawed pimp, more tar than mammal and more dog than man. "Examining time," he was apt to say as he inspected his girls for flaws. The Barghest was, after all, a businessman. And like all businessmen, he had learned of the new Food and Drug Act passed by "that walrus of a president what had made everyone sell quality to the people." The Barghest was no fool. The Barghest would sell quality to the damn people. The damn people wanted whores like water, but the whores had to be quality.

"Jessup, darlin', this is the year of Jubilee. You know? The year of Jubilee. The Barghest turns fifty," he said through whiskey-laden laughter and cigar smoke. He was red under his black skin, glistening in his own sweat.

"Well, happy birthday to you, then?" Jess was little impressed with the Barghest, though he had been her boss and her pimp for somewhere near ten years, now.

Her breasts bounced when he asked her to jump up and down. His bulldog jowls filled with smoke, and he growled. A happy growl. A trumpeting of triumph.

"Got a kiss for me?"

"Is it your birthday yet?"

"Your skin's puckered underside of your thigh. Have Alma get you some cold cream."

Before she came here, Jess would wander in the crevices and rafters of barns, burrow in with the mice and be as small as small could be. Jess's Sir was a white man, who her Ma'am said was filled with passion but little love. This Sir was a ghost. He did not appear in anything but half-hushed stories told between adults. Like *hope*.

She remembered the day that word rolled off Aunt Mizzy's tongue and the mousy girl couldn't seem to even breathe after she said it. Jess was hidden in a rat's nest in Aunt Mizzy's parlor, half-sleep, while her Ma'am was cooking with Aunt Mizzy for church come Sunday. Aunt Mizzy said the word, and it struck Jess, as Aunt Mizzy seemed too old to believe in fairy tales.

When Jess and Ma'am went home that night, she burned with the question.

"Ma'am, what's hope?"

"An old dangerous thing that lurks in corners, Jess. I'll tell you when you're older."

"Is it real?"

Jess's Ma'am paused for a moment. "I can't tell much about it, darling. Hope takes change. And only the sea can change."

The Barghest had said when they had met: "Oh, Jessup, baby, I can change. Just like the sea. And watch me! I'll be someone new tomorrow."

And she wanted to believe it all too much. Believe that someone could change; that anyone could.

The Barghest did change, in fact. She saw it happen, that first night. She watched the molasses smile for customers change into a hardened snarl by night's end. If Jessup had learned fear, she would have run in horror at the sight of the Barghest that first night. But she had never learned fear, because she had never learned hope, either. Her Ma'am forgot to tell her. By now, Jess had known the Barghest to switch between sweet lapdog and fell beast so often that the word *change* could not remain in her vocabulary. She had seen him greet a customer with a smile and then found him gnawing on the man's bloated remains only an hour or so later.

A sudden commotion at the back entrance shocked Jess out of her mind. Some of the other prostitutes were giggling and shrieking and racing across the whiskey-warped floors.

"Must be that piano man," said the Barghest. "He never is quite on time. Always a little early or a little late, never on time."

"Can I go now?" Jess tapped her bare foot on the floor. The piano man's arrival meant she'd have to squeeze herself into that gold velvet dress for her habanera dance.

The Barghest waved her away. "Make sure Alma brings me my dinner into the office."

The Bramble Patch, the Black section of Napoleonville, came alive on Saturdays in a valley of iniquity called Mercer Street by the city officials and "Mercy City" by everyone else. Mercy City was where the hot music aroused and the hot women slept. Rag-music peacocked and strutted out of every bordello, bar, and dance hall and into the street; a great moaning and hollering paraded down Mercer Street. And that clash of those two noises was dangerous to passersby. It was a well-known fact that no one passed through Mercy City without some siren ensnaring him or some piano man calling to him with a melody.

Tonight, the world would be filled with only the music and moans of Mercy City, though the Christian soldiers would shoo away the devil if they could. They never seemed to be able to get him out.

Esther Lyons leaned quietly against the red brick spine of the New Jerusalem AME, pressing her body against the cornerstones. Until the brick would snap her back in half. All she could see was the New Jerusalem, shining with marble banks and white houses: the white side of Napoleonville, up the hill from the Bramble Patch. The longing crept into her bones, to venture up the hill to the white side of town. In her hand, rough from hours of peach picking, sweat pooled and tarot cards crumpled. There, in the crooks of her knuckles, the paper cut into her. But she was to fly into the solitude of New Jerusalem, ooze into its shadows like a streak of sludgy tar on a hot day; those white people wouldn't suspect a thing if they saw Esther Lyons, because she would be a tarry shadow, flecking herself on the little white clapboard houses. Because she knew what was coming to Napoleonville.

Esther was so scared, she laughed.

"Repent, brothers, repent," she called to a hustling group of men, but as they murmured their reply, she heard the nits in their hair chatter back and forth to themselves. She didn't hear the men. They were heading to Belladonna's place, the crooked blue building that leaned too far to the left. The nits clicked and clacked over the men's talk, blurring the natures of each. Man-nits—nit-men—all the same as far as she was concerned. She was concerned about it very little.

Esther wasn't proud of her mind that filled the gaps between tomorrow, yesterday, and today. Ma Lyons wanted her to get out of the house and join the crusade, occupy that mind with the rightside up, instead of the sideways and upside down. Pastor Mose told Ma Lyons that it would be wonderful to have Esther hang out on Mercer Street some Saturday night and "stop our men from fooling around." But what he really wanted to say was, "Thou shalt not suffer a witch to live."

Esther eyed around the corner to see her mother preaching to Yeoman and Jack. She oozed back into the shadows and towards the Barghest's place. She knew her mother agreed with Pastor Mose's thoughts.

The burnt end of the day sunk slow into the horizon. Slow, to where the Barghest's ladies crowded around the back alley to take a smoke break before they danced. There was blood in their veins, for now, Esther noted. They had nothing left to fear, for the Barghest had told them what he was. There were no more demons left, for now.

The piano man rubbed a dancer's arm tenderly as she adjusted her threadbare robe over her corset and chemise. This one was called Ida. Esther watched it happen, feeling the man's heart thunder in his chest as his mind filled with images of both Ida and Jessup, with him. Esther was the tar shadows, watching it all.

"Wiggle for me! Shimmy and shine, girl."

"Don't!" Ida pulled away and took a long drag of smoke.

"Girls who smoke don't have class, sweetie pie."

"Haven't you heard, mister piano man? No one does."

The piano man plucked the cigarette from her lips and took a drag himself. "What you want wiggle to tonight?"

"Nothing the Barghest wants to hear," slender Fannie broke in.

"Shit, try me, woman. I got his balls, Fannie. Without me, he's just a two-bit barker without a pony to show for it."

Ida glanced up at Fannie and then across at Winnifred, who nodded. Ida whispered into the piano man's ear and nibbled on it a bit. He wilted at the knees.

Esther wiped her free hand across her pinafore and strained to hear more, but the burning eyes of Jessup, watching over the other girls, brought her to cowering. She felt Jessup everywhere at once in the alley. Esther did not like feeling watched. Especially not here in Babylon. Not by Jessup's burning brown eyes protecting the other girls from the piano man. Esther went back to the wooden sidewalk out front for her evangelizing.

There Danuel strode by with Ernest, hot-mouthed and horny already. Their sons swaggered behind, giggling. Poor boys. When the war would come, and it would, their brains would break and they would live out their days begging for scraps, while lesser men than they could've been would get rich watching them suffer. Danuel's son would be due for a lobotomy in forty years' time.

Esther reached out to the boys. "Repent," she whispered. The sweaty, crumpled tarot cards fell to the ground, and her knees hit it too, before another word could pass from her lips. Those boys were like corn on the stalk. Ready to be plucked and shucked and mashed and cooked and popped. Her hands trembled at the thought: Repent. Repent. For the kingdom is nigh. The end—sooner.

When the Napoleonville schools would be forced to integrate, the Bramble Patch would slowly die, drained of people, and fade to a historical marker on the side of the road. The Bramble Patch would become undead. Most of the land would be overgrown and turned into a twisted, jumbled forest—the sign would be a marquee for ghost stories. There would be no more stories about Doctor's nephew stumbling around blind drunk on Saturday night and leading choir Sunday morning. Jessup's breast, barely concealed under gold velvet, would no longer fill the whispers around the cracker barrels in Marion Chapman's store. Marion's store would be shuttered when the Kresge would come, and Marion would die when he hung himself in the cellar storeroom.

Esther trembled, knowing that history was coming like a stampede, and that when it had trampled over the Bramble Patch, only headstones would remain. Headstones and perhaps the Barghest. He seemed to be timeless, collapsing the very idea that all things must crumble into the sea, wither, and die. He would gray slowly, drinking blood like wine.

"Shit," said the Barghest. "Shit. Shit. Shit."

Blood dripped from his bloated jowls onto his newly starched shirt.

"Shit. Listen to that music," said the Barghest to the pile of black limbs on the pewter plate. Arms and legs like blackberries juicing blood—black skin crushed into crimson.

"Listen to that music," said the Barghest. But the ears on the plate were deaf now. "Piano man's playing slow. Too slow. There's gotta be bump and cake walk and grizzly bear. How else they gonna wanna make love?" The Barghest set down his hunk of thigh meat and listened.

Beneath the tiny patterings of a phalanx of mice galloping across the floors, the piano man was playing soft, rolling the melodies of an operetta off of his fingers and into the air. The Barghest could smell the first cigars of the night being lit, as the men who came for the girlie show were starting to settle into their seats. He knew a few would doff their bowlers and dust them off. They would clap hands and laugh a little together and start ordering drinks from Sam. And soon he would have to go down and introduce the girlie show and tell his girls which laps to sit on and which to ignore. Despite having eaten a few of his customers, the Barghest had a very loyal crowd. A couple of men, Ernest and Danuel, had been ushered into manhood in this house and had brought their sons after them when the time came.

But if the piano man wouldn't play hot music, then how would the men want to drink and watch the girls dance? And if they did not watch the girls dance, then how would they want to burn through their money for a night of pleasure? And if they did not want a night of pleasure, how would they come back again and again, week after week? And who, then, would satiate his hunger?

He remembered his Sunday School teacher, Miss Alice, giving the word of the Lord. "A certain stevedore is walking through Jerusalem in the Promised Land. He sees this old brick theater in the city. He hasn't eaten in days, for he was a poor man, poorer than any of us will be. So the stevedore, he licks the side of the theater. Earth—red earth—fills his mouth. And when he ate that brick dust, he felt his muscles grow a little. Curious, he ate more brick dust. His arms got thicker. He ate more. His stomach grew stronger. He ate more. His legs never grew tired. He ate even more. But then, his skull got thick and his mind got slow and his heart got hard. Soon he ate so much brick dust that he was a brick-man. Brick-man can't move. Brick-man can't breathe. Brick-man is dead. What's the lesson, my children?"

And all the children thought and thought. And then a little girl named Faith said, "Anything that gives you power has power over you."

"Amen and amen," said Miss Alice.

Now, at fifty, the Barghest knew what Miss Alice had meant. She meant the piano man and his music. He grabbed his kerchief and wiped the blood from his mouth.

In a moment or two, he would go down and introduce his girlie show. He would have Ida and Alma flirt specially with the doctor and his nephew. They came every other Saturday, but a lot of sickness had ravaged the town of late. The doctor needed a break. The piano man could be murdered after tonight's show, while everyone was too drunk or too sexed up to notice. Then the Barghest could put the best parts of him in the icebox. Tomorrow, he would find a new piano man.

UNTITLED

After the piano man's forearms were eaten, Esther began seeing a girl in her dreams, in the golden reflections of brass kettles, in rain puddles splashed up by mules, in the grease stains on Marion Chapman's apron, in the kick of heat in her mouth when eating pickled peppers, on the bully stick Officer Dean carried when he made his patrol. But mostly, Esther saw the little tar girl when she looked at the Duncan Farm and saw her father and brothers and cousins and friends and nephews and uncles out picking grapes and peaches. This sort of thing was why people thought Esther was touched in the head—gaping at the peach orchard and grape vines like that for hours instead of doing anything else.

Out there, her little tar girl was in full focus. All unseen in the haze of heat, she black as tar, naked and bathing. The sweet smell of black soap scrubbing the body into strands of flesh and mud, and palm ash streaks darting along the belly, which bore a scar—from when her belly was slit open to save her son, priced at her entire life. She died bleeding out while her husband, more than twice her age, congratulated himself on having a son. She was thirteen or maybe fifteen; the grave marker wasn't so sure. Younger than Esther, anyway. She stood in the rows, verdigris under the shade, naked and bathing, unaware of the hands working around her—mostly because dead people, in Esther's estimation, did little and nothing to notice the mechanizations of the living. The little tar girl just bathed. Scrubbing black soap across her scar until it burst raw with her own blood, but she never seemed to notice. Sometimes, while the rivulets rolled down toward the folds in her hips, she would start singing an old song, singing: "I know it! 'Deed I know it, Sister. I know it! Dese bones g'wine rise again."

But mostly her naked ghost would stalk the minute and quiet parts of Esther's day, making as little noise as possible, showing up in the smallest moments. Barely a ghost. More of a whisper, a murmur.

Murmurs shattered parlor windows on the white side of Napoleonville in the home of Paul and Susan Dougherty. The newly installed Tiffany glass was found strewn about the floor in shards, for the rumor had busted in with such force it shook up the house. The story was that the Minister and Mrs. Jonah Kincaid had hired a Negress to watch their children. Not just any Negress, either. When Susan asked her cook about the new girl, the cook said *tsk* and *shame* enough to make Susan worry. The Negroes said the girl was touched and stood around staring at the Duncan property every day like a cow whose leg don't work.

Mrs. Kincaid, who rarely kept darkies around, had encountered the girl Esther when her mother delivered some brocade robes, hand-stitched the old and quaint way, for Founder's Day pageant costumes. She noted her slight demeanor and pleasant smile. She examined the small finger bones, the pops they made as Esther lovingly traced the leaden outline of Christ in the window. Plain enough to not invite temptation. Quiet enough to prepare the small ones for a life of charity.

"Do you like the window?" Mrs. Kincaid asked.

"Yes, ma'am," Esther had replied. She immediately became aware of the fluttering heartbeat of the moth in the corner. Esther had never even been to the white side of Napoleonville, let alone talked to a white woman before.

"What do you like about it?"

"The colors of the sash." A regal purple and blue, fluttering splendor of the resurrection all splayed out—unlike all she had seen, frayed woolen cloak of poor craftsman, which she knew Christ to be. "You got colors like that in New Jerusalem?"

"Our Second Coming window is the third to the left from you." But Esther had not meant the windows. "Does your daughter like children, girl?"

Ma Lyons suppressed a sigh. "Well enough, ma'am. Esther always a help with her cousins and brothers and sisters. Now her little niecey, too, these days."

THESE BONES

Esther could see the little tar girl on the corner across from the church, naked and bathing and humming in front of the schoolyard for white children. The white children all played around, dancing and jumping rope. A boy shot a marble that rolled to her feet; she kept scrubbing her skin away, turned and waved to Esther. Through the purple prism of Christ, Esther recognized that kind smile of youth, open-mouthed and hungry, ready to rip the children's innards out. The heartbeats of moths were silenced as the little tar girl, now scrubbed clean and soaked in her own blood, walked across the playground with soap in hand looking as though she meant to clean the children playing unaware. And that was when another woman, tall and broad-shouldered and also black as tar and naked, but carrying a basket atop her head, followed the girl, swaying her hips to the hum of the song: "I know it! 'Deed I know it, Sister. I know it! Dese bones g'wine rise again."

Esther's silent smilings struck Mrs. Kincaid as contemplative, a trait she found to be rare among Negroes. That there was the end of it as far as Mrs. Kincaid was concerned.

Esther hummed the tune: "I know it! 'Deed I know it, Sister. I know it! Dese bones g'wine rise again."

THE FUNERAL

Out by the Negro cemetery, the matriarch of the Bramble Patch sat on her porch, regarding the town from her seat.

Before Time itself, 'Livia Marvell had been sitting there. She was older than mountains, the folk said. She watched the trees grow from seedlings into forests; she held the stories of this place in her blood. But this summer was laden with memories like fog filling her lungs. Her daughter, Mizzy, stood behind her, braiding the white crown of kinks and coils. Snowy tendrils floated into Mizzy's hand.

"You're shedding, Mama," she said.

'Livia didn't answer. She clasped her bony hand onto her daughter's wrist. "I ever tell you 'bout when I was in that tintype?"

Mizzy nodded.

It was during that bloody war—Mr. T. Duncan's brother, Mr. S. Duncan, and his nephews and cousins were fighting for the Union. That April, that day, that moment was etched into 'Livia's sinking suspicions of the world, almost creating them from scratch. The grand house as it once was, sun-baked with auburn wallpaper and Persian rugs. The bunting, tied up pretty. Every moment stuck in her mind as a reminder of the ruins of mankind. What if Judgment Day was near?

'Livia looked up at Mizzy and told her to lean in close. 'Livia's whispers burned into Mizzy's ear; susurrus fear sent shivers through her. Later, at Ida's funeral, she'd tell the church ladies about it. Most of what her mother said sounded like lunacy at this point, and the church ladies knew it. The rambling of an addled mind, nothing more.

THESE BONES

'Livia said: "I saw a white man talk to that one nigga, the one with the whorehouse. 'Cept the white man wasn't any white man. He was the devil. I swear, the devil. I saw him as I see you now. Saw him just like he was, the devil. And that boy asked him for all the splendor of Solomon in his life and to have the time to accrue it. To stay young and beautiful as long as it takes him to be a rich and wise man. And everyone knows: the Barghest hasn't aged since. It's been forty years and he ain't aged more than ten. I swear it. I swear he and the devil have a thing going."

Mizzy laughed.

"It's funny, see? Funny," Mizzy told the ladies at the funeral. "She doesn't know what she's talking about." But in her chest she felt a pain radiate from under her ribs.

It takes many hands to make a funeral. Someone to clean the body and bear the palls across the plain wooden box. Someone to talk to the white folks in charge; that was the hardest part. Someone to call the kin up from the worlds beyond. Someone to feed the people. M'Dear and Silas and their boy, David—that's who wrought the chthonic work of death in the Bramble Patch.

"They found Ida's body cause they heard a scream," M'Dear said as she pitched the remainder of the powdered sugar atop her lemon cake. "A scream so loud, it shook the whole street loose." Lemon cakes cost too much, but under such circumstances, it only seemed fitting to make a few.

"I just can't—this doesn't happen in the Bramble Patch," remarked Honey, one of M'Dear's two helpers, as she raked the fiftieth apple with her paring knife. Apple crumble was cheap as anything. It was the least she could do.

M'Dear sucked her teeth. "'Course it happens here. It happens everywhere."

"Who screamed?"

"One of the other girls from the show. Winnie, I think? They say she saw it first."

"Heaven! I just—and Winnie's such a sweet little—I just don't believe it all."

"Believe it. Believe it. Pastor says he saw it when they—"

"Pastor? Pastor saw it? What'd he—"

"Hush up and let me talk. Anyway, he tells me the body looked gray as dawn."

"Here in Bramble Patch…suppose what the white folks'll say?"

"I don't know. Sheriff Dean's already looked her over and left."

Honey stared down at the bucket of apples at her feet. "Where's Nell? Ain't she supposed to help with these—Damn. I just can't believe—Ida have family?"

"Miss Matilda's a cousin. Ida's parents died a few years back. Then again, I'm only going on what I heard, but I know she doesn't have any other family near here."

"Suppose it's better that way then. It sours a soul to hear this. Here in Bramble Patch…"

"I got the lemon cakes done. I'm going to start on the potato salad. Gimme a hand?"

Honey would not be distracted from the whereabouts of the other assistant, whom she suspected of malingering. "Where is Nell?"

"Stop being antsy. Nell's probably at the church, setting up for the funeral. Can you help me with these potatoes?"

"Ida doesn't have folks but we're making all this food?"

"Honey…"

"I'm just saying."

"What are you *just saying*?"

"Didn't have family. Killed herself."

"Hush up and peel these potatoes."

Honey stood silent for a breath or two. "Who's gonna come to the funeral of a whore anyway?"

"I wager there'll be more than'll be at yours."

Honey snorted. "More than yours, still." She grabbed a small knife and dug out the curved eye from the potato in her hand. "Why, though? Why'd she—"

"I really don't know. Winnie said she might have fell in love with a john or such. Not sure. Sours a soul to think what drove her to it."

M'Dear rubbed her knuckles against the table. Of all her funerals, this one was filling her with the most dread. Her old bones seemed brittle and dry, falling into the despair of years. How many funerals had she and Silas managed? How many mornings were born in bright hope only to be drenched in mourning and condolences? How many cups of coffee and how many lemon cakes and how many apple crumbles had she made for the bereft? How many women in town had she paid from her own purse? Women like Honey—thrice a mother, twice a grandmother, and once a widow. And Honey, who still buzzed with the nerves of a giddy girl—how many times now had even she done this?

This was not about Ida's body. M'Dear had grown accustomed to every kind of body in all manner of death, violent or not. But the face—the twisted smile, left over from Ida's last thoughts—she sewed it shut, and yet the glee of rest remained on the corpse's lips, as if the simple act of remaining alive was a sham and true delight was in death. That night, when M'Dear went to bed, telling Silas about her day at the funeral parlor, she found herself asking what manner of man the Barghest must be if this little girl was smiling in death. Now that memory nipped at her heart in a frozen place.

"M'Dear? D'you see her right away? D'you see her in the tub, I mean?"

"No. I went after Pastor and them. They were the ones that brought her to the church. I went up, though, and the Barghest hadn't even drained the tub."

"What'd it look like?"

"Red. Just…red."

Perhaps her own eyes in the mirror, perhaps the pitch darkness of night, perhaps the cool hand of a john, perhaps the soft whirring of the pendulum clock, perhaps the last dregs of coffee in a tin mug, perhaps the flood of Ida's blood filling the bath red, perhaps the ink on the corpse's fingertips, perhaps the frost-rimed grass some morning last March, perhaps the crystal of her Habanera dress, perhaps the curse woven into the corset, or perhaps the stench of the piano man's remains in the icebox—perhaps all of those pieced together in a row—pushed Jessup's heart to sickness over thinking about the Barghest.

Down below, in Mercy City, the men were leaving for home, as dawn peeked up over the hill. Kicking Jess's love down the road, they were laughing and tumbling in the way only intoxicated men could. In the way that spilled forth into disaster when they would truly awaken. Danuel, especially, clapping his son's back. Danuel's sloppy souvenirs from the night—the trace of lipstick, the stiffness in his groin, the laughter in his eyes—would disappear into the light. And Jess would be watching from her tiny window in the whorehouse.

Her ma'am spat the word with venom. *Whore! Whore! Whore!* She sang that refrain, over and over, clapping to the beat. Jess liked to giggle a little at the word, pretending it was nonsense noise.

"Jessup!" he barked from his office.

She muttered a simple curse to herself in the back of her throat.

"What you say?" he yelled as if he could hear the thoughts pounding in her head. It was just the headache behind her eyes; without the cool damp cloth to rest into, she just pushed her head against the window.

It began in this way, pressing her forehead against the cold window, watching Danuel laugh. And hating the Barghest. The Barghest and his smile like fire in the reflection of the piano man's pupils. Hate twisted her stomach. Hate churned her innards. Dashed upon the quiet hill of torment in her own way, she was brimming with that bile. Then the bile leapt from her throat and onto the window.

It wasn't the first time. The first time this happened, her mother had called her a whore for the first time. Jess had prayed it would be the last.

"Jessup, get up here!"

The blessed child, she decided, would be named Wanhope.

Esther Lyons was keeping track of her charges' misdeeds.

The glass of buttermilk was filled with carpenter ants, scrambling over each other in a panicked daze, screaming the noiseless shrieks of drowning, while JJ Kincaid, the second son of Reverend and Mrs. Kincaid, watched with a silent smile and licked his lips.

Croswell Kincaid—aged four—kicked a sleeping hound. The hound stirred only an inch or so before sinking back into slumber. Croswell Kincaid—aged four—kicked the dog again. The hound sighed heavily and dreamt of rabbits on the mountain. Croswell Kincaid—aged four—kicked the dog a third time. The hound sank his teeth into the fat of Croswell's face, leaving him droopy. The hound was shot over by the gardener's shed the next morning.

Penelope sang and skipped rope. Penelope played Beethoven for her mother's bridge club, hymns for her pastor's sermons, carols for her teacher's Christmas concert. Penelope embroidered roses and truisms onto pillows. Penelope wrote in her diary about going to the state normal school to teach little darkies to read and write as a missionary's wife in the jungles of Africa, next to the dirty pictures she kept of Sandow the famous strongman. Penelope flashed a glimpse of her burgeoning breasts to the neighborhood boys for a nickel.

Samuel, the oldest at thirteen, always smelled funny. He smelled like sulfur and Jessup's perfume.

Daily, as Esther watched the children, the two naked tar women stood by the windows and sang their song. Esther sang the song to the children when she put them to bed.

"I know it! 'Deed I know it, Sister. I know it! Dese bones g'wine rise again."

FROM *A HISTORICAL SURVEY OF NAPOLEONVILLE* BY EUGENIA KINCAID (1912)
Chapter 11: The Negro Population

According to township records and census maps, Napoleonville's Negro district down the hill, known colloquially as the Bramble Patch, was built on the trampled remains of land belonging to R. Miller

Croswell. You will recall that the Croswell family were among the first of our Scotch-Irish pioneers to settle this land and that R. Miller, in particular, was integral in founding the Napoleonville school and library after his gristmill business flourished.[1] While the Croswells were initially successful in their business, the devastating flood of 1830 left much of their land infertile. This, coupled with the tragic death of his sons Micah and Evan and of his first wife, *née* Sarah Winston,[2] led to R. Miller's eventual abandonment of the land.

The Bramble Patch comprises a few streets cross-cutting the swath of land formerly belonging to the Croswell family. The major thoroughfare is Freedom Avenue, which is a tributary of sorts from Napoleonville's Main Street, meeting the main artery of Napoleonville. Running parallel to this are Asher and Lincoln streets, where several prominent families of the Negro race inhabit modest houses. Most of the surrounding area is a shantytown.[3] The few cross streets are Mercer, Perry, and Harris. Rural routes extend from these.

---

[1] Note from the 1976 edition: Eugenia Marietta Croswell Kincaid was a cousin to the R. Miller Croswell family and may have exaggerated his contributions. Contemporary reports indicate that R. Miller Croswell was no more integral to the establishment of Napoleonville than other well-to-do men living in the area between 1810 and 1845.

[2] Note from the 1976 edition: Referenced in Chapters 3, 4, and 14 as death by typhoid, but after her death and even until Eugenia Kincaid's time, rumors persisted that Sarah Winston was murdered.

[3] Note from the 1976 edition: Most of this land is now overgrown, and nothing of the historic "Bramble Patch" remains.

FIGURE 11.1

No one is sure when the Negroes first began to settle in what would one day be known as the Bramble Patch. However, the neighborhood's first major building, the African Methodist Episcopal church, was erected in 1841. The original edifice burnt down in a fire the following year; the brick church which stands in its place to this day went up four years later. This was made possible thanks to the contributions of several fervent missionary spirits in Napoleonville, including my late father-in-law, Samuel Wilkerson Kincaid, pastor of the Napoleonville Second Baptist. It should be noted at this point that several Negroes had been a part of the initial settlement that became Napoleonville, but they did not live in the town proper. During and after the War, the town's Negro population grew. The accompanying tintype (Figure 11.1, above) depicts some servants of the Duncan household, including the Negress Livia Marvell (center).

LAUDS; OR, A MORNING MEDITATION

Friday, June 13, 1913

Penelope lifted her knees to her head. Esther held her breath. Penelope pearled her body up into the parlor rug and, catlike, eyed the blond woman and boy coming up the path to the house. Her eyebrows, lips, and back arched a little. Esther felt insatiable hunger burn her lips. It was not her own but Penelope's. The sun hung a little too close to the grass, and Esther placed her hand upon her stomach, hoping to rip out her guts. It was morning.

And with the blonds, there was a brown-haired man, trailing a few steps behind. He half smiled like he had just remembered a private joke. There was a flurry of linen and dotted cotton as Penelope brought herself to attention and ran to the door.

"It's not proper to accept guests this early, Miss Penelope. With your mam and father gone, too."

"Lower your eyes, darkie!" Penelope said. Esther turned to liquid and sank into the wall. Penelope leapt at the door. Energy quivered inside the foyer. "Peter!"

The man Peter smiled with an ever-increasing air of obligation and greeted Penelope as "Sistie." Esther had seen him a few times before, at the home and at the church. He was a friend of Samuel's from college. Peter was older than the Kincaid boy, twenty-one to Samuel's seventeen. He had a straight back and a tongue that lay crookedly between his teeth. The blonde woman next to him smelled like raspberries and too many other people's fingers. He and she, they were spitefully good-looking. Esther knew that the man's surname was Ailey, and that his mother called him Dob as his first name was really Peter-Robert. The woman was his fiancée; her first name was the same as some virtue that white folks pretended to care about. The boy between them was pale. He didn't speak; he was the Virtue woman's brother, but she resented his youth.

Peter wanted to know if the folks were home. Penelope dripped onto the doorposts and shook her head. Esther stood looking at the Virtue woman. Down in the yard, the tar women were bathing naked, singing their song over the lot of them. The Virtue woman had plaited hair and a little Brownie camera.

Peter eyed Penelope. Virtue and her brother stood silent. "That's a shame, Sistie! We needed to talk to your father."

Penelope shook her head again.

Peter would come around Sunday, then, after church. Virtue and the boy had to go home tonight. Just like the song Mrs. Kincaid played on the piano, "Catch the Ten Fifty-Five to My Henrietta Love."

Esther heard the hammers inside strike the piano strings and saw the tar women reach out.

It *was* a shame, Penelope noted. She dug her nails into her palms. Crescent moons of terrible scarlet bloomed in the soft flesh. Only the blond boy noticed and he balked like a mule. Esther saw the tar women begin to split their mouths open in laughter. Penelope stalked her eyes over the Virtue woman's entire body as a breeze cut through her white linens and raised her skin. Then she declared the coming picnic and dismissed the group on the porch.

Peter Ailey and the others—Verity, the fiancée's name was, and her brother Jerry—left. The church bells began to ring. Verity and Peter stopped to take a couple of photographs of a little home down the street. They planned the names of their future children and what sort of furniture that little white house would hold. Jerry asked for a picture of the draft horse in the adjacent field; Verity obliged. The three went back to a small hotel room.

It was too bad, thought Esther. Too ugly. The tar women had touched his blond hair, and it was now marked with their sticky splotch. They were still laughing when she went to the back kitchen for bread. The sun was too low in the sky. The tar women sang their hymn. There was fire in the river already.

THESE BONES

A NEWSPAPER CLIPPING FOUND IN REV. JONAH KINCAID'S OFFICE

Letter to the Editor, New York Herald, *1913*

Can it be said that America is falling prey to the collective soul of the Negro through the influence of what is popularly known 'rag time' music? If there is any tendency toward such a national disaster, it should definitely be pointed out and extreme measures taken to inhibit the influence. This music is symbolic of the primitive morality and perceptible limitations of the Negro type.

FROM THE DIARY OF SAMUEL KINCAID
WEDNESDAY, APRIL 23, 1913

She's a nice shade of periwinkle when she smiles. She smiles pretty and I like the bloods in her neck. She shudders breath and rains silver from her flat bare feet. Sings from her hips "honey," which drips on my lips. I could plunge my hand into her cavities and pull out her gallbladder and hold it at night.

I want to. I want to.

Is this what a man feels upon falling in love?

The harrowing tremble of her frantic heartbeat while you walk behind her.

I think she's seen me walking behind. I want to sink my

teeth into her hand while I kiss it. She's chocolate candy and hysteria. This is my madness and my slavery.

How do you get to the Bramble Patch? When your daddy's the preacher and your nurse was a Negro, too? Maybe you wish you had a black bastard over in the Bramble Patch.

I don't miss standing in the back of their peep show, watching them devour her. With her baby, they don't want her, and I can eat alone. How do you end up seeing her and wanting to set your own body on fire to prove that she's your own shade of periwinkle? I want to crumple into the flames and jungle music. She's threadbare and whelped—yet I adore her.

I dream she's at the edge of the river, rocking my aching head back and forth; I dream her breasts and the trees are whispering in the wind and they tell me to gobble her tongue and I do and I swallow her blood and tears after and she thanks me with her eyes and baptizes me in the cool of her body. I wake up in Onan's shame.

I watch her walk overcanted, smiling and turning periwinkle. Honey waits at her hips.

MARGINALIA

Following the river behind the little white boy named Croswell—he held his sister's doll by fistfuls of hair, the smell of mischief dripping from him in pools of sweat, as if summer weren't ever a good idea—Esther's brain pulsed with the river's current. Esther liked to drink switchel, which was molasses and vinegar mostly, on hot days like today so she could feel as sticky as the mule who pulled the ice wagon. Instead Mrs. Kincaid had packed up canteens of water for Croswell, JJ, and Penelope. A smallish tin cup for Esther, who carried the basket through the woods. With Samuel away at seminary, there were fewer eyes on her these days.

Penelope didn't mind her brother clinging to the doll's hair, desperately dragging her through the forest, but Croswell's teeth clacking from his over-pronounced overbite drove her to sprint away. There hummed with the bees a sort of drowsy springness, drowning out for Esther the humiliating vision of Penelope's future peep shows in a year or two as she would grow from girl to woman with sinister smiles. Penelope for her part slowed to a lope not too far ahead and sank into her own gray eyes. The Reverend and Missus were taking Samuel to a tent meeting in a place far enough to be called "away" but not enough to be called "far." Penelope had the Reverend's eyes, which was why Esther feared her the most, or maybe it was her rolling tongue, begging for the satisfaction of kissing older boys and men. Or maybe it was the cloudiness in Penelope's future beyond a year or two.

When Croswell asked Esther why she looked so sad, she lied and said she missed 'Livia Marvell. No one really knew how to miss 'Livia, not properly in the way she deserved, least of all Esther. The Marvells for their part hissed nasty rumors between the pews at church—that Ma Lyons was a whore and Esther was the devil's punishment. In the trains heading back down South, there were whispers about a little Black witch living and working in Napoleonville, trembling in the clickty-clack-clitckty-clack on the bridge that crossed the river a little to the west.

Esther almost told Croswell about the train cars tumbling down into the river, the fire, fire, fire, burning the water. She repeated the phrase she'd heard gray-haired aunties tell each other: "It sours a soul." Croswell wasn't cruel like the others, she reasoned, just naïve. And naivety could be just as damaging. If not more.

The electricity in the June heat shocked Esther's tongue, zagged into her soul. She was left suddenly naked; each layer of her body peeled away from the rest. Frayed, she felt the tug of the tapestry around her, a single thread pulled out to the rotting guts of tomorrow—maggoty with the stench of blood and silt. Her eyes hit heaven before plummeting back down to the margins of the wooded path and a spot up the creek.

Further up the creek, a blue-black dot skipped against the horizon. Even from this distance, Esther could make out the braids splayed out in every direction, like epidermis sliced away from fatty tissue. She cringed and cringed again, looking at the baby, Wanhope. There, trailing at Jessup's skirts, toddling behind her mother's hem, leaning against her leg, clutching shards and wrinkles of the gingham dress, which Esther could see was made roughly by hands with too many blisters. So clumsy and swollen, the hypocritical fingers of a new laundress and an old whore.

Esther hadn't seen it happen, but the ritual of lactation had made Jessup's body impossible. Her breasts had sat atop the boning of her corset like overripe peaches whose skin split with boozy nectar, sweet and hot to sting the throat of the suckling masses. But something about the burst was ugly, patrons complained to the Barghest. Matronly. So Jessup had left the corset on the bed she once worked in and taken the toddler to Honey's house. She left the corset because she was neither whore nor lady anymore but something other entirely.

Sometimes, at night, Jessup's heart fluttered between her ribs as she remembered how she was once adored. It scared her, how neatly the jagged little line split her world into a double realm. Until that day she left, the difference between adoration and indifference had seemed like the difference between night and day, but in reality it was the difference between flotsam and jetsam, the difference between New Amsterdam and New York.

TIMETABLES

THROUGH TIMETABLE EFFECTIVE JAN. 1911
Passenger Train No. 17

Northbound-Daily	Station	Southbound-Daily
Noon	Marion	11.20 PM
12.25	Napoleonville	10.55
1.00	Webber Junction	10.20
2.00	Jericho	9.20
2.20	Ilia	9.00
3.15	Braunstown	8.05
3.50	Henwen	7.30
5.00 PM	Tullulah Acres	6.20 PM

HYMNAL

Yonder Come Day. Mama's made of cotton trailing in the pricker bush and mud. Knees—pink. Eyes—too tall for me. I stick my hand in the apron pocket. Nothing. My eyes hurt. My mouth wails. My eyes are wet.

Wanhope. Hush up. Yonder come day.

The bottom of her hand is made of white people skin and spider webs to hold her together. No sweets in the apron pocket. Prickers on her knees. Thorns grow from her thumbs—*Mama, up*—the thorns are in my scalp.

Your feet dirty. Don't touch me wit 'em.

Mama, down. I'm back down to mud and grab the speckled skirt.

Don't ask me to pick you up again, Bit. Yonder come day. Day done broke.

We leave the river. We leave the trees too—Mama and me. Hair's wild and the dress slips off brown me.

What color? I pointed to me. *Brown.* Mama looked down with her tall eyes. Mama's eyes got wet.

She's a shepherd like Jesus. What's a shepherd? Why is Jesus one? Why is he a good one? *Mama, why Jesus good?*

She smiles. She shows teeth. *He's so good, Bit, cause he God. Day done broke. Oh my soul. Yonder come day.*

After the river and trees comes the street. Eyes look at me. They are so tall. Mama's sad. My hand's in her big one. Eyes look away. She sings louder.

Yonder come day. Yonder come day. Day done broke.

The people are all brown here on the street. By the river, they're white too. Some of the doggies are white. But their eyes aren't too tall. Just right. Mama's made of apron made of feedsack—smells like chickenbirds. Chickenbirds are scary. Chickenbirds with eggs are mean. Chickenbirds got thorns on their feet. *Mama?*

Hmm?

I want to say chickenbirds are mean but I remember they taste good. *Chickenbirds taste mean.*

Mama spills laughter from her mouth. I feel my tongue. Mama is shimmery in the sun. I want to love her forever. I want her to never stop shimmering.

She had soaked in the washtub. She had smelled like roses. She put my hand in her big one when she wore blue.

What color, Mama?

Baby, baby blue, Bit. She spilled a laugh. I loved her.

It was a dress. She took me to the street. Took me to the sagging place. Took me up the stairs. And then the door open. There were other women—they were naked mostly.

Mama, they naked.

Hush up, Bit!

Then there was a man. He was brown. But he was black too, black from his belly. I smelled salt. I smelled black.

Wanhope—you wait here. I gotta talk with the Barghest.

I put a mouse's hand in mine. I sat near the door. Mama disappeared behind it. I was hearing them. The mouse and I were hearing.

What's wrong with you girl?

Found God.

You got religion?

Don't.

I know what a revival looks like. You found God the way I found a hundred dollar this morning. You might've needed it but you didn't find it.

You know my Bit? I need you to take her.

How I know she's mine?

THESE BONES

If she ain't yours, she's your fault.

You were a whore what got pregnant.

I was a good one for you, you know. I did what you asked. Sexed 'em and cooked 'em, too, and didn't tell nobody.

You won't neither. You're rotted out. Gone bad as can be.

Who made me that way?

We all make ourselves. You liked dancing and sexing. You came to me for the work. You ain't gonna peg me for that. And you ain't gonna leave your Bit in a whorehouse.

Mama came back.

Bit, get off that nasty floor.

We left the sagging place. We walk past it now.

Yonder come day. Day done broke. Sun is arising. Oh my soul. Yonder come day.

Mama smells like what the river hides.

Mama what's the river hiding? I looked down.

Flathead catfish and Negroes.

I looked up. *What's Negroes?*

Mama's eyes got wet. *You, Bit. And me. And all the folks in the Bramble Patch. All the brown folk. Not all of you. But enough.*

There's King and Ma Lyons and Dinah and Lazarus and them others. Mama never says them's names, but I know my numbers to ten. There are four thems. Them are wild.

Mama, what's wild?

Them Lyons children. Them wild. But so's the trees at the river. They just grow and grow. No one touches them. Untouched. That's wild.

Them, they hang on the porch and smell like pressing comb oil.

Ma'am. Mama calls Ma *ma'am. Where's Esther? I wanna see her.*

Ma Lyons looks with tall eyes but she's sitting in a rocker.

She's working for the white folk today.

King smiles and shows his teeth to me. King is a Papa. King is good, too, so he loves Jesus and Ma Lyons and Esther and Dinah and Lazarus and Them. But the teeth in his smile look sad.

Where's her stuff? Ma looks at me.

At my place, still. You can get it from Honey.

Didn't you hear the bells? I reckon Honey gonna be gone all day.

Mama's tall eyes look down to the mud. *I still gotta pack mine.*

Them go to scare some chickenbirds. Them aren't touched. Them scatter into the four thems. Them get loud. Lazarus follows. He's brown now but all of him is gonna be black. Black and blue. Black and red.

You ain't got to, Jess. It don't have to be this way.

I got God now. Mama gets into the apron pocket. It's a paper. *And I got someone too. Preacher's wife can't have other kids. What'll they say?*

God knows, though, Jess.

King, you take Bit's hand.

Ma Lyons's eyes go to Mama again. They get taller. *He knows you. He knows what you been. Who you are. Who you birthed, too.*

Mama turns her eyes to me. Her lips are in my braids. *Wanhope, you better be good. You better. I'm going to write you. And maybe in time. Maybe in time. I love you.*

Mama looks leaky. Mama looks down with her tall eyes but now they seem so small, so black like the man in the sagging place. King puts my hand in his. His makes mine small, but Mama's eyes are still smaller. I want to swallow up the mud at the back of Mama's skirt. I want Mama. My eyes are wet and I want Mama.

Hush up, Bit!

She know you leaving. You think she don't but she do.

Bit! Quit crying!

I want Mama but her eyes are only ants, black and wriggly. And they are going down away from King and Ma Lyons and Dinah and Lazarus and Them. And me. Brown me sees brown Mama turn black along the drive, back to the road. But I can see the bottoms of her hands and feet still. I see the sun burn a hole inside of forever and the wild of trees and Them. That's what Mama's made of.

ALL

M'Dear had never cried at one of her funerals. But M'Dear was still cleaning 'Livia's body, cleaning the crusties from her eyes and spittle from her lips. Nell and Honey were cooking in the back room. M'Dear was cleaning the body in the front parlor; Silas had long since lost his stomach for death but his name was still on the funeral parlor sign, which read "Silas and Sons" even though they only had one son. She was rubbing the sweet wrinkly forehead, smoothing it over and over and over and over with anointing oil, hoping to erase the spots of age. A hint of pepper hid in the decomposition of the body, now. Maybe stories would spill from the creases in her forehead: the Duncan Brothers' secrets, tales of the Barghest's youth, the War, how to make that butter cake, the winter that the cow got froze to the barn, the lyrics to half the hymnal, how to get prickers out of the kinks of a baby's hair, the last traces of the mother tongue that the Bramble Patch ever knew. M'Dear was old enough to remember when she was Olivia Marvell, when there was no such place for Negroes called the Bramble Patch, and the woman called Olivia could speak some tongues and would say they came from Africa; she tried to teach them but they wouldn't listen. Then her tongue twisted over the words in exhaustion so she kept silent. M'Dear was also too old to remember much else about those days except that they seemed stitched of vibrant hues of purple and blue and the brown of the people. M'Dear felt torn, as usual these days, hovering between the nostalgia of a time before the Bramble Patch and wondering if such a time had ever been.

'Livia's daughter Mizzy's folk all the way from Ilia had arrived by wagon and mule already. Mizzy's sister and brother-in-law and nephews and her Aunt Fortuna and Cousin

Miles, carving their way across the backroad stretches between here and there. Cousin Miles was cracking his knuckle bones while he and Mizzy's brother-in-law broke out a game of bone-sticks at her table. Aunt Fortuna was his grandma, but she was smaller than his own children back in Ilia. Miles could have pulled the wagon hisself, thought Mizzy, and she laughed for the first time that day. Mizzy's sister and brother-in-law and nephews and Miles all laughed for no reason but that it kind of ran out of their mouths, too. Aunt Fortuna was quiet, remembered when Miles was so small he couldn't pull the wagon and they came to visit. Aunt Fortuna told him what the river hid: mudcats, Negroes, the tears of their mothers. She asked Mizzy where Jessup was now and Mizzy was mostly unsure. Only mostly, though.

There was such a time as before the Bramble Patch, Grandma Ady recalled. But it was mostly before her time. 'Cause her voice sounded like rain on hammered tin, most people wouldn't listen to her too well. Grandma Ady was nearly blind but she could still darn socks with wild bucking stitches. She could remember the stitch just as she could trace her fingers across the ugly swath of earth and remember that this home was once a neglected plantation. She was listening to hurried footsteps outside and recalling the world from before. She didn't know it well, but 'Livia had. And she was gone now. Grandma Ady's hand tremored suddenly. That was the thing about 'Livia and her people: they were too melancholic and too long-seeing, could remember the times before and after and all the things that were in between. 'Livia's fingertips and DNA remembered the seasonings of Port-Au-Prince, from a time when she was yet to be born. Her body remembered the malarial visions of her ancestors, passing between dream and reality as you might pass from the door to the porch back and forth on a hot June evening.

When the Reverend Jonah Kincaid packed up the Model T with his wife and eldest son, heading down a little bit west for the tent revival that weekend, he felt a strangeness under his tongue. Not in his gums or jawbone but on the lingual frenulum, which had been cross-cut with his own knife years before. He was trying to prove a point– God as healer, Jehovah Rapha. *God will heal me*, he shouted to the group of boys. He fell to his knees and put the knife to his tongue. God would give him speech again. Mouth bleeding rivers, he cried himself into tear blindness. A shadow loomed into scales over his eyes. And wrinkled hands grabbed the hinges of his jaws. She was black as black had been to a little boy. She cradled him close and lifted him into her arms. She prayed over his tongue. He spoke again. Jehovah Rapha.

First thing the morning he left for the revival, he went to his office at the church to pin the news clipping to the wall. He hated himself for loving the devil's music. He hated himself for pressing his ear to hear the music from Mercy City. One of the Duncan boys knocked on the door—Miller or Georgie; he couldn't tell them apart—and came in saying that 'Livia

Marvell had died. The Reverend had only ever known two Negroes that he had liked and 'Livia was the first and better. The news didn't make him sad per se. But that night, as he watched his eldest son Samuel dig his fingernails into his own shoulders, praying over and over and over again for forgiveness—"Guide me, O thou great Jehovah! Deliver me from my lusts"—he almost felt a little sorry that 'Livia was gone. No better Negro would he ever know.

All along the thoroughfare of Mercy City, evening had settled into the back of everyone's throats; it had cut a swath into the back fields at the Duncan Farm. No one meant to get bluesy in the Barghest's beds. Blackness settled on the Bramble Patch. Not the star-studded velvety cool of night but the limp blackness of mourning. It hung upon everyone's shoulders. Except the Barghest; he just kept grinning too big.

Jacob Jonah "JJ" Kincaid leaned his forehead against the glass of the bedroom window. The cool of it made him choke back tears. Or maybe it was the way his darkie sang "Catch the Ten Fifty-Five to My Henrietta Love." Cousin Whit Croswell had sold that song to a Remick's a couple years back. Mother played it at the piano, and the darkie liked the song, and he liked his darkie. He knew it in his bones, sickly and sweet. And when Penelope said the other darkies said she was a witch, he wondered if she could weave him a spell. And if, once woven, the spell would travel from her lips to the ears of the devil and make it real. If she was a magic woman, why wouldn't she use magic to make herself white?

JJ was the one who caught Samuel in the twisted sheets of orgasm, who ran to Mother in disgust, who asked Samuel why he kept having vile thoughts, whom Samuel slapped bloody, whom the darkie bandaged and cooed over, who wanted to know why those other ones thought her a witch. He growled Penelope's name as the cool window throbbed pain through his head. She didn't want to be called Penny anymore but Sistie only. He wanted to know why the darkies thought his darkie was a witch when she seemed to be etched from fine black marble, and though she was nearly twenty, older even than Samuel, he wished she had been etched from white marble instead. He wanted to have those same vile thoughts that Samuel did and the same twisted sheets, and he wanted to tell Penelope that Peter Ailey was practically married and that she should—

At that moment, the 10:55 train to Henrietta failed to make it over the bridge.

The whole town shook as the train tumbled and crumpled into the river. The engine leaked. The river was on fire.

AUTOPSY

The tongue is too black. The heart is too silent. The meat is boneless, the mind is scrambled, and blood pools up nearest to the kicks of flame.

The wrought iron is curved and twisted like the spine of the little blond boy splayed against what used to be the caboose. The miracles outpace the discoveries of finality—a scream, but she's alive; foot mangled, but he's still breathing. The stars blink slowly, the skin roasts evenly, the blood drains into crepe de chine and linen. Seersucker. Straw from hats. It's summer, after all. A dying hand trembles. A dead tongue lolls. A train's whistles lilts and then screams. The remains of an eye are smashed in the gravel. The iris is frighteningly gold. No one will remember who in town had golden eyes.

Splashed against coal was a Negro woman. Or rather both halves of her. The difference between the two halves of her body, hemorrhaging in convulsive bursts, marrow oozing out from her severed ribs, was the difference between New Amsterdam and New York, between Constantinople and Istanbul, between the Bramble Patch and an overgrown plantation.

FROM *THE AUTOBIOGRAPHY OF RHYTHM AND BLUES* BY CLIO COOK (1972)
Chapter 8: "Black Magic Woman"

I turned the Nova down along a dirt road that twisted like the metal frame of a car wreck. The radio was hovering over words and snippets of music and then would return to the crackle of the static. It was good for my headache. The night before, I had ended up at a pool hall. Folks'd see me and say, "You're not from these parts." I'd tell them about my little book, the men I'd interviewed, all the places I'd stopped. A couple of the old-timers told me I needed to go to this place called The Crooked Nailhead and talk to a man named Bobwhite Teller. My heart raced at the name; I remembered it from the faded blue label on my dad's record. I told them thanks, and then I slammed back a few bourbon rickeys, 'cause it's hot down here.

In the back of the station wagon, I caught a glimpse of my favorite pair of boots, the vinyl crinkled up and more than a little sweaty on the inside. The shoes reminded me of last night's mistakes. A blister grew under the canvas of my Chucks, and the remnants of my hangover drummed inside my skull.

As darkness fell, gravel kicked up and flipped at the windshield. Fireflies lit strips along the highway like I was landing a plane. A couple of times, I stopped for the haunted, hollow eyes of deer galloping ahead of me. The disc jockey turned on "Black Magic Woman," my ex's favorite song. I tapped my fingers on the steering wheel and there it was: a shack pulsating with light and music.

The Crooked Nailhead was the kind of roadhouse where they still throw peanut shells on the floor and you can get cheap beer in a frosty glass and a cup of ice chips to throw down your back. As I dragged my recorder into the place, I saw I was the only white face in the sea of black ones. The blue plate special for the night was fried catfish, cornbread, and greens. All the tables had been moved to one side to make way for the dancing—there wasn't much of it, though. There I was, with my tape recorder and my pen and paper, looking like a schmuck.

Up on a set of risers was Tommy "Bobwhite" Teller, whose frail body seemed to barely hold up his Dobro as he played "Let's Get Drunk Again." I muttered to myself, "Let's not." The old man wore a bowler. He would tell me later: "There was an old pimp back home who wore one of these. When we were kids, we used to want to go to his place to buy a night with one of his girls. Got it in my head that's what you wear when you're rich. I never got rich, but I still dress like it."

He moved his fingers across the guitar's neck as though caressing an old love; he picked at each string as though listening for its story. He played with a cigar stuck between his teeth that seemed bigger than his head. Bobwhite tells a good story with his body. When he finished playing the song, he walked off the stage to a little stool and drank a Seagram's 7 on ice.

He propped up the guitar on the bar top, and I could see him shaking as sweat poured over his thick-lensed glasses. I walked over and introduced myself. I told him that I used to listen to his singles until the grooves went bleary. The bartender handed him a plate of catfish. He sort of shrugged his shoulders. "I get tips, fish, shit else these days," he said.

"Where'd you first learn how to play like that?" I asked.

Bobwhite smiled in such a sad, crooked way that I didn't understand the belly laugh that followed.

"At Tempess's place," he said.

"Tempess Place? What did the name mean?"

"Place didn't have a name. Didn't need one."

"So then who was Tempess?"

"Tempess was tall and dark. Swayed into the room like cattails on a breeze. She wore pants and riding boots and a tie. She smelled like pine tar; when she kissed you, you would close your eyes and find yourself in the embrace of the undergrowth. When I think of Tempess, I think of laughter sprinting out of her big red lips. And the stark white girl who trailed her skirt."

He placed the ice-cold glass against his forehead and let the condensation roll down his face for a moment. The folds and wrinkles in his face said, "I miss the high of something sweeter now." He threw himself back into his chair and threw back the rest of the Seagram's.

"Shit, girl, you must be a long way from home! Where you from again?"

What can you say to a legend like Bobwhite Teller? Do I say Brooklyn or that I studied at Vassar? Do I tell him about the shtetl my great-grandmother grew up in or about the summer place up in the Catskills? Or do I tell him about the room with the record player, in the brownstone, where my father would pull vinyls down from a shelf so high up I couldn't see it and say, "Ah, now this one, Clio, this is a classic"? Then the needle would touch the grooves and the hum and crackle would begin as he crumpled into the rocking chair.

But Bobwhite Teller moved on.

"I'd bike down to her place with my fiddle. Cross the bridge from the Bramble Patch. There'd be the river folk on the other side. And a shanty made of tin and cardboard on a dirt patch. It'd be me and my best friend. He was the piana and I was the fiddle. We'd hightail it in there, because we was always late. Between schoolwork and church and chorin' and seein' the Barghest's girlie show, couldn't make it on time. But Tempess, she didn't care. She was usually a little drunk, go up to everybody and give 'em a hug. Even our late asses.

"Once we start playin', the place was shakin' with dancin'. That's when Tempess start dancin' and kissin' on folk: men, women, it never mattered. She had her little girl with her. White like spider silk, we called her Moonchild. I got to askin' once where Tempess got a white baby from. She just laugh. All she ever did is laugh at anything: joy, sorrow, pain, hate. A white lover, she said, from Jericho. She laugh again, and said, 'I seen him and something came tumblin' down, and it weren't a wall.'"

"What happened to it? Tempess's Place?"

"Prohibition took the booze away. The Depression turn the songs to sorrows. Then a flood swallowed up the shack and Tempess, too. You can't know what the river hides and not expect to tempt fate."

"A lot of things collapsed after the Depression."

"Not the Barghest. The old pimp stayed moneyed."

"Well, the oldest profession and all that," I noted.

He looked up at me with squinting concern. He muttered something about his damn cigarettes. As he clawed into his pocket, I couldn't help but think about my dad holding up the Bobwhite Teller 45s wrapped in fading paper. My dad, leaning over me, smiling with a cigarette in his mouth. I was really young—my mother had died not too long before, and my aunt was finishing Shabbat dinner. Ash fell from my dad's mouth as he said, "This right here! It's like a diamond, Clio, a diamond in an effing coal mine." I handed Bobwhite one of the cigarettes from my pack. He smiled and continued.

"Me and my best friend, we'd play anythin' we could think of: spirituals, marches, hillbilly music, songs we heard old-timers sing. But always in a ragtime style-like. My favorite was this old, old song, 'Darlin' Cora.'"

His voice warbles and warps but finds the right tune as he sings.

> *Child, dig a hole in the meadow*
> *Dig a hole in the cold, cold ground*
> *Child, dig a hole in the meadow*
> *Gotta lay my sweet Cora down*

I smiled a bit. For the record, based on things he told me, there is no chance in hell he was singing that song in 1921. The earliest known appearances of the song were in 1919. But he is nearing seventy, and years of hard heroin use haunt his fingers.

"Was this in your hometown?"

"Bramble Patch?" he asked as he lit the cigarette. "Bramble folk didn't think of the river folk as belonging to us."

"Bramble folk?" I asked. For some reason, I felt uneasy.

"From the Bramble Patch," he explained. "It's been gone a long while. That's my home. D'you ever—" He looks at me dead in my eyes as tears start to form in his.

"You ever see the sulfurous smoke of hell, Miss Cook? How it rises up in black billows and consumes everything? I have.

"That pimp had a crooked evil smile and blew black smoke from his nose. He come to Tempess's place once. She was getting better business than him. He come down there to scream at her. He told her, 'How you gonna take my customers when you ain't but river folk?' And she called him a bitch. She said, 'Ain't you a little bitch!' He raise his hand to slap her, but she spoke and the wind thundered in the pines. Her voice moved the river; the waves crashed against the Barghest. We stopped the music. Silence. The wave scattered into his face. His suspender slashed in the wake of her curse. Yes, the Barghest was made ugly and bullish. Where that little bitch belong. His bones shuddered in anger. We heard 'em rattle. Tempess said, 'Get the f— out my place.'"

I was ordering a second round for myself by this point. He's gotta be pulling my leg. Our eyes met and I searched for the wink in their shine. But there was no wink. There was no shine. Only quiet. Which was only broken after the catfish was gone and the tumbler was empty, when the great Bobwhite Teller was picking at the remnants of cornbread.

"The pimp stared me down, I swear. Me and my best friend. The smoke and sludge of hell, he took with him back across the river. Fire belched from his footsteps. Him, fire; and her, the water. Nothing could stop either of them. So they moved through our world, and we let them. But they made us. They sustained us. Until they didn't. Then they swallowed us whole."

"What happened?" I asked. We were leaned in so far.

"Come on, Miss Cook, you're smart! There's always water and fire. Soul and bone. My best friend and me. The holy and the wicked. The Bramble Patch and Napoleonville." He put his hand over mine, and his voice dropped to susurrus timbre. "There is skin and sinew. There is this second and the next. And between those, there is a long stretch of breath and stillness and potential. So to answer your first question, that's where I learned to play music."

I laughed and let go of his hands. He hollered for another side of greens as he drummed against the bar top. My stomach felt uneasy. I stood up to leave, but his calloused hand grabbed mine again. He looked past me into the neon glow of the sign outside. "All of that is a memory these days. The wisp of smoke at the death of the flame. Tempess spoke and the waters parted. She belonged to the river. She and hers belonged to the river. And the river took her. The thing that she was consumed her. I think about that a lot these days."

He was about to play his second set of the night, so I went over to the payphone to check in with my baby sister, Markie, before it got too late back in Brooklyn. The hesitancy in her voice told me something was wrong.

"Your damn ex keeps calling," she said.

I groaned. "He's got some nerve calling you."

"Well, he told me to tell you to call him at home once you get back to your hotel."

"I'm staying at a motor lodge," I huffed.

She groaned. "Doesn't matter, Clio. He said it was urgent."

I groaned again. "Fine. I'll call him back. Oh, and Markie? Tell Dad I got to talk to Tommy Teller tonight."

We exchanged a short goodbye and the homey twang of the Dobro started again. "All right, had my fill of catfish now," Teller said. "I'm gonna start with an old song I loved called 'Darling Cora.'" He looked at me and smiled.

But I, for one, felt a wave of dread hit me. So as he picked away at the guitar, I silently slunk out the door with my recorder and my notes, just like the black magic woman slipped into the flood waters of a river she was made of.

When He separated the waters, God said, "Let there be sky and river, and let us gather the gully from the river and make them different, too, and let us scatter the coal-black seeds 'til they find deep, good soil." God tossed them down the river, and they lined the far bank and rooted themselves into the islands and marshes and all the way to where the river was dammed up. And Bertha's kin sprang forth. They were older than the earth—grown from the formless waters that God spake into—and shooting up from the mud like cattails in the river islands.

Bertha was infolded and calloused from crown to sole. She'd been a slave in the time before, had come up from a place no one knew the name of. She said, "Was the mouth of hell." She never spoke of it again. Folks used to think her kin was from the Carolinas. But it was a "might be" tale.

There was a lot of "might be" tales about Bertha's kin. Folks said you only go down to Bertha's kin during the sad hours. When the grass turns blue under a hazy moon and your own sorrow, when you've had to drink corn likker to forget and there's not a single girl at the Barghest's that can satisfy you. You go to Bertha's kin when your man's been creeping at midnight. Folks said the little dwarf man knew voodoo from down in the tropics. You go down to him— Bertha's grandson-in-law or nephew or something—and he will brew up something with chicken blood and a lock of your lover's hair. And make you drink it. Then your man will come back shaky and all-overish with glassy eyes, lovelocked to you and cursed. Some nights, there was a panicked holler that came out from the reeds across the river. Folks said, "Isn't that the sound that comes from skinning a cat?" Folks in the Bramble Patch said she and hers did the devil's work. But what folks didn't know is that Bertha was the patron saint of lost things.

No one noticed shadows or the swirls on lost mother-of-pearl buttons, or the mottled skin of bent sewing needles, or the little brown girl lingering in the reeds. Not her bright scarlet dress or her braids born of battle between scalp and comb. But the gray eyes of Bertha took in all of these small lost things. She smiled toothlessly at Bit. The weathered hands reached out among the foliage and pulled up the little girl in her scarlet dress. "You lost, little girl?"

Wanhope shook her head, her lips plastered over in fear.

"You sure?" the old woman asked.

The little girl wasn't sure. She was willing herself to become one with the reeds and the cattails and the water and the amphibious skin which clung to her little brown legs as she stood barefoot in the water. She was not far from her house; she could make out the dusty remnants of her own footsteps leading back. But she felt in her guts a wave of uncertainty that clawed at the rugae of her stomach. Her words were small then, but when her words got bigger and they put an MD behind her name, she would know about the chasms of her body into which that pang was nestled. She wasn't far from her house, she knew that very well. But she found that she was lost from home.

Bertha took the girl out of the water. "You don't belong to the river, girl. You belong to something else entirely."

"My mama told me what the river hides."

Bertha plopped Wanhope in the mud and snarled. That level of foolish talk smacked of something sinister, smacked of her granddaughter's arrogance. But this child wasn't their kin. Maybe it had been Rhea's open maw that put such ideas in the heads of the Bramble folk. Lord knows how Rhea could—

Then Bertha looked into the child's eyes. "Oh," she said with a quiet nod.

Long ago, Bertha had asked the river for life, but life got to repay life. She had run to the river; the river hid her from the white men. But nothing could hide her from the river. So she gave the river what it wanted, if only in necessity. To give the river something out of cruelty was to tempt fate. This little girl wasn't for the river.

It had been a strange summer. The seeds of the cottonwood cloaked the ground like snow. This little girl belonged to something in between the Bramble Patch and the river folk and Napoleonville.

"What's your name?"

"Wanhope, but most folks call me Bit."

Bertha walked with the little girl along the banks of the river. And the world was just those two, like broken glass in shattered spangles. The lost things headed somewhere familiar.

TEMPESS'S PLACE

The Bramble folks called me Moon-child. Nowadays, I go by Ma'am or Selene. My milky white skin hides me in sunlight.

My man's hands trembled when I told him. He couldn't tell, of course. I'd be surprised if he noticed. White folks never know what to look for. And I've done my best to disappear and be reborn as one of them. But I'm from here, too—the side of town he dreamed of as a boy. My folks' side of town.

He smiled and kissed my hands and said, "I guess you always belonged here."

How could you think I belong to Napoleonville? The white folks in town were always cruel to me and my kin. Home is where the stones grew like moss over the ground and the river belly-laughed as the icy waters danced.

I slept during the days, letting my scalp sweat kinks into my auburn hair. Mama didn't send me to town for schooling. All the reading I needed was a menu. All the arithmetic I needed was keeping Mama's books. Night would approach and, like a wedding procession, they would don their best. Not their best clothes, mind you. So few of us had good clothes back then. But their best crowns of joy sat crooked upon thick, coarse braids as they chasséd down the dirt path. I'd press my nose against glass to stare at them. In the halo of dusk and the fog of my breath, they were iridescent. Azures and scarlets and blushes and plums and honeys waltzed down the road, effortlessly royal. I did my own pigtails and put on an old cotton dress, nearly gossamer with age, and I'd go down to greet them and take their entrance fee.

You knew you were close to Mama's place when you saw the oak tree that grew crooked at the fork of the dirt path. It was over the hill from there. And once you were over the hill, it was pretty easy to spot. The gutters shook with the hoots and hollers and stomps. The windows pulsated with shadows. The ground trembled when the door split open, breathing light into the darkness.

The smell hit you first. You could buy a bag of fresh donuts for a dime, covered in wild honey. They were still warm and greasy in the paper bag. No one made hot donuts like Miss Phoebe, who was short and always wore a mourning dress since her husband died. She would fry up bacon sandwiches, too, for fifteen cents. If we were lucky and could get the Poles from the city to come down our way, Phoebe would serve kielbasa and mustard on rolls.

Peanut shells carpeted the floor. Mudcats swam against the current just to hear the songs inside. Most of the time it was the Teller boy and the Lyons boy playing tunes. But sometimes, if we were lucky, it was that Jug Band from east of here. The washboard and jug start shouting at the guitar and banjo, and the banjo and guitar would answer back. The night became hurly-burly on our side of the river. Gaslight and piano, laughter and hooch poured out of the windows and doors.

I just laughed behind my lips, not wanting to be heard or seen. Mama sat above it all and moved through the throng the way some folks say the Holy Spirit moves through a body. 'Til you're dizzy from sacred electricity glowing in your skull. She walked through the room and breathed air into everything. My mother dispersed into a million atoms of stardust and would glitter over the crowd. And I was scared that if I laughed too loud or spoke up, the spell would break and this court would disperse back to brambles and dust on their own side of the river.

There was no shame, no need to hide. I needed no mirrors of glass; I could see my own joy in the smiles of everyone around me. I could gather my skirt and feel the bones of the world creaking under my feet as we danced. And we danced every night 'til those beautiful black and brown faces melted from sweat and ecstasy and the sun hovered lilac at the horizon. One by one the procession of everyone disappeared behind the trees. The waters stilled in the morning. The mudcats hushed. And I would achingly crawl back into bed as the sun stood rosy above everyone.

You knew where you were when you got there.

You were home.

THESE BONES

SWEET AND SOUR

The Teller house sat at the bottom of a hill that graded down in a lovely swoop. In those days, that house was whitewashed, and the curtains billowed and swam on the breeze from the open windows. The Tellers were one of *those* families: the ones that lived on Asher or Lincoln Street and wore spats and satin ribbons.

Little Tommy Teller, who is supposed to be practicing his fiddle in the good parlor, is eavesdropping on his sister and his grandma. Like on every Saturday night, the tug of the comb wrenches Bessie's head back into Grandma Ady's knees, which are like the old knobby stories that keep children from squirming too much. There's as much cartilage in her knees, says the doctor, as there's branches on a loblolly pine. He's from the Carolinas so he talks funny. One of Bertha's folk.

She slaps Bessie's ears and says, "If you stop moving, it won't hurt." This is a lie, by the way. But it's the lie her mother told her and she told Bessie's mother and Bessie'll tell her daughter. All Black girls will hear this lie at some point.

Next to Bessie, Miss Matilda is snapping beans—bending the springy greens and snapping them with the pressure of a heated quarrel between lover and lover or father and son. Bending them the way Bessie imagines God spoke the universe from the void to the snap of Creation that exploded across the sky from His own mouth. Next to her, Mother is darning socks, worn through by her baby brothers. Grandma Ady tugs through the tangled mass on Bessie's head with the comb. "You tender-headed as anything," Grandma Ady reminds her as Bessie pulls against the grip. Grandma Ady's eyes hold visions, reflected in her cataracts, as she begins to twist the strands at the scalp.

The canter of foot-foot-stick, foot-foot-stick, foot-foot-stick comes up the wooden sidewalk as Bessie wiggles into the porch. Her behind is numb; her feet are tapping out a different rhythm in her shoes, the ones she's already outgrown but must wear for another year. There at the porch steps stands Mrs. Harris, whom the old folks call M'Dear, but Bessie calls Mrs. Harris. She is trailed lovingly by Nell. Grandma Ady picks apart the husks of hair fiber by fiber. She doesn't look up.

"Afternoon, Ady. Girls," M'Dear begins.

"How's Silas and 'em? And August, Nell?"

"Fine, just fine. Ady, what you bringing to the church picnic?"

"Not going."

"Now, Ady, come on!"

"With this rain? My rheumatism? Almanac said it's a cold, wet autumn."

Bessie recalls when she ate from the prairie crabapple, thinking sour was a type of painful sweetness yet to be discovered. And when she vomited the acidic bile in floods and floods until Grandma Ady gave her horse chestnut, which she used for everything. The horse chestnut is good for the following ailments: Varicose veins. Fever. Menstrual pain. Swelling.

THESE BONES

Eating sourness and calling it sweet.

"I'll give you the recipe for my cream puff so you can make it, Nell."

"You got it writ down?"

"Not this one."

Bessie pulls away from the hands weaving and plucking at her wiry hair; some rips from its roots, and she hears that over the sound of:

"Quart of flour, then smattering of butter. I like to use a wooden spoonful, but it don't even need that much."

The wind weaving through the trees.

"Now you wanna beat them pretty good or the bread'll all be too eggy."

Tobacco leaves drying in their bushel baskets.

"A gill of cream and then the yeast. I usually let it rise over-night when I make a batch that big. Then a teacup of water."

Grandma Ady's knuckles cracking as she braids.

"Half an hour in a hot oven should do the trick. Depends on how much you making."

But she doesn't hear anything over the edge of weariness in Grandma Ady's voice, which hovers in the air after she speaks, a slight apparition. Like hammered tin or shattering glass. Like the Aunt Nancy stories Mother told at ten-thirty by the grandpa clock in the hall. Like milkweed rustling with dormouse intercourse, like silky blue stockings hanging from the line, or like the way the sun peeked out from the clouds but way too close to nighttime to matter.

"Bessie, grown folk's talking to you. Answer 'em," Mother's voice snapped.

Bessie had heard; Miss Matilda was talking about her history report.

It had been about when white people first came. She and her brother had put "In the Land of the Pilgrim Fathers" to music. Miss Matilda hums the tune, and Grandma Ady weaves another taut line down Bessie's scalp and tells her to sing it. Not without Tommy, she thinks and almost musters the courage to say so.

"Lazarus Lyons played the piana for it, too," says Miss Matilda.

"Huh," says Mrs. Harris.

"He's good at piana."

Grandma Ady stops braiding. "He work at that place for Bertha's kin, don't he? Out in the marsh?"

"Mama, you know King and Dove ain't proud of it," Mother says.

"But they too proud to stop it."

Bessie calls for Tommy to bring his fiddle to the porch before the tsking and teeth sucking starts.

Bessie imagines Tommy having to hide his fiddle so he can go play at the juke joint tonight. But right now, he brings the fiddle to the porch and they begin the duet. With Grandma Ady's weaving fingers keep the beat. They smile all. They smile too large for their faces. And in her barely cobbled shoes, in her black stockings and cotton drawers, in her starchy chemise, in her pink dress that's shrinking as she grows, under her pinafore that pins her to childhood, next to Matilda, snapping beans next to Mother, on Grandma Ady's porch, Bessie recognizes the exhaustion in every word.

NAPOLEONVILLE LADIES' LUNCHEON CLUB NEWSLETTER
DECEMBER 5, 1918

Hometown Hero Spotlight

Dear all,

Thank you for your kind letters. It was nice to know that I am in your thoughts and prayers. Being away from my wife and our little girl has been so hard, but fighting the Hun was my patriotic duty and now fighting shellshock is my other one. This flu is knocking men flat on their backs to the grave, and the ones that do survive the sick… they have a lot to worry about otherwise back here in the hospitals in Washington. You all give me hope.

Regards,
Peter Ailey

PHOTO OF MISS EMILY BOOT'S SCHOOL

1918 Christmas Charity

For this year's Christmas charity, we will be donating to the Negro Waif's Home in Tallulah Acres. Our Christmas charity coordinators this year are Mabel Hastings, Dorothée Keith, Winnie Dougherty, and Eugenia Kincaid.

This year's charity takes care of Negro boys from around the county who are either delinquent, neglected, or orphaned and puts them to useful trades such as animal husbandry, musicianship, gardening, carpentry, and trades for their future endeavors.

THESE BONES

Flowers of Spring in Dead of Winter
A Poem by Penelope Kincaid

Flowers of Spring, leap skyward!
Though the sky be dark with gloom
Do not tarry towards sunlight
For the sunlight lives in you

Dead of winter may scold you
And rebuke you towards the dirt
Flowers of Spring, go forth
Away from your mother earth

Flowers of Spring in Winter
Are bound to show their faces
And bring with them God's glory
Even in the darkest places

KAYLA CHENAULT

My sisters you are the flowers
That cover the earth with green
So grow in the dead of winter
You wond'rous flowers of spring

FROM HEARTLAND MELODIES: INSPIRATIONS FOR BLUES STANDARDS FROM MIDDLE AMERICA

Abstract

The common cultural narrative of blues standards is that they originated in communities of color in larger American cities, especially with the contributions of artists from the Northeast corridor. The history of this music is strewn with "anonymous brute[s] 'n boo'ful buck[s]," to borrow from Ralph Ellison. This narrative, however, erases the role Middle American artists played in the early formation of the genre. The lack of Midwestern exploration in existing historical surveys means that many active sites of inspiration for the melodies remain unaccounted for. Just as Marion, Indiana, cannot be divorced from the legacy of the jazz standard "Strange Fruit," many works by noted blues artists drew inspiration from Midwestern environs.

THESE BONES

Tata Duende, former circus curiosity and father to a girl nicknamed Snow-baby, was pushing Snow-baby's pram with stuttered gait into Marion Chapman's store. He was followed by some of his wife's folk: Tempess and the mixed child, called Moon-child, at her skirt. Tempess had her grandma's eyes, like his wife and his baby; those eyes were the words that told the "begat" story all the way back to Adam, Auntie Rhea said. Tata Duende could not see his baby's face in the carriage, but he knew that she had a star-kissed face. He used her freckles to make constellations. Tempess laughed behind him as he cooed at the girl. She laughed because she thought he was foolish to think that child was his. She wasn't small like him, and she was a tint above snow. Tempess laughed until she noticed two dull eyes peering out from Marion Chapman's store down to Mercer Street. And she glanced into the eyes of the Barghest, half-cataracted and humbled a little now that jazz was floating from her juke joint in the swamp down into Bramble Patch. That made her laugh harder and harder. Her piano boy was young and had good hands.

Tempess's glance shifted away from the shuffling coon up the road to the little boy down the road. He was Tommy. Tommy nodded to Tempess and Tata Duende but skirted on by to his friend, Lazarus. Talked to him about Lazarus's girl, Bessie. Bessie was smart and good in school, like her beau.

She was with his child, too, growing bigger. She had a beautiful voice and wanted to sing with her man later that night but wasn't allowed to. Lazarus wanted to go to the Negro college in the fall, but Bessie hoped he would stay for the baby. Tommy said all of this to Lazarus, because Tommy was Bessie's brother. Lazarus just nodded slowly and left Tommy on the road. The curtain of heat rose and Tommy trotted back into his mind and played the chords he had heard Lazarus play so often.

Lazarus was walking down Freedom Road, the path he had traced in his veins from childhood onward. At the crest of the hill, Freedom Road would turn into Main Street and the whiteness above it. This road had scarred him across his legs, which had switchbacks of tissue raised from a caning. He never liked it here. The ground was hallowed. The earth was still burnt out from the train that passed through but never left. This was sacred, holy earth, between the black and the white, between the Bramble Patch and Napoleonville.

His neck was bulgy and ringed in sweat. Sweat drenched his spectacles so he couldn't see the spot where Jessup's body was found split open. Daddy King and Ma Lyons couldn't afford the glasses, but he had a white benefactor up the hill who was interested in Negro education. And now Lazarus could wear the spectacles he had needed for so long and could play real piano music away from hully-gully drunks and maybe could go to a Negro college. His benefactor said white folks were willing to invest in an industrious Negro.

In Lazarus's hand was the sheet music for the concert that night. The crows kept screaming at him in the trees. His sister Esther was a witch, the folks all said. The crows followed her, and her kin. Still, she'd gotten him the white benefactor. And how it went was that Daddy King sent him to go get her from the white Reverend's house where she worked. He had just started working in Tempess's place and Ma Lyons didn't like it because of the sexing and marsh fever. Ma Lyons said to him, "Not all poisons come in vials and snakes. Not every poison is made of things. I named you for someone who come back alive. Lazarus, son, don't ever go anywhere you can't come back from. Don't get down a path that don't lead back to alive."

But he had nimble slender fingers that could memorize tunes on the piano against all odds: son of a peach picker, son of a seamstress, son of the Bramble Patch. He liked books and carried them with him everywhere. He went to the Negro school, even though all Them worked and Dinah and the witchy one, too. He liked words. He liked music.

He met the white benefactor because he went to get Esther from the Reverend's house, and he took a book with him. That amused the Reverend's wife, because she thought she'd never met a Negro that liked words. She thought the whole lot of them were curiosities.

And she asked, "Are you looking for a job?" And he said, "No ma'am." And she said, "That's odd, I've never met a

Negro boy not looking for a job." And he said, "I got a job, ma'am." And she said, "What's that then?"

He looked at his sister, but she would not look at him. "I play piano."

"What sort of things you play?" asked the Reverend's wife. She placed her hand on the head of her child.

Esther's face contorted in disgust. Lazarus said, "They're hymns of a sort."

"It's just as well, then. I know you don't know any of our hymns. We took your sister to the church to watch Croswell. She didn't know a single word of them. We're Baptists."

"Yes, ma'am."

It was then she decided a Negro boy who liked piano and liked reading needed a benefactor. To save him from the Bramble Patch. Everyone thought him to be the best of them all.

Now he rang the bell of his benefactor, Mr. Richard Keith, and heard a voice say, "Well don't just stand there like a dumb cow." It was the benefactor's daughter. He winced. His hair was combed and parted but his lips were swollen from a bee sting. Dinah collected honey and had asked him over to watch her kids. The benefactor's daughter had disdain dripping from her own lips. The sheet music shook in his hands. He walked inside.

Down the street a house or two from the Kincaids, the blonde woman was perched up on her porch, half-mad but beautiful still. She was Verity Ailey and she wore her hair in ringlets. Beside her, a little Black girl held a cup of milk from which Verity drank. Long ago but not so long, Verity had boarded a night train, and now her right hand was gone. She kept the stump wrapped up in a crocheted shawl. She had lost a brother too, and she kept a piece of him wrapped up in the shawl as well. Her husband passed by and grazed her cheeks with his lips. She didn't look up to his eyes, but the little Black girl did. Her name was Wanhope, and she was reading Dickens to Verity on the porch. Verity half heard the book, half remembered language and how the tongue connects to the mind. Her nerves were half severed and half forgotten. Her eyes remained fixed on the spot where a draft horse had grazed seven years prior. "Girl! Take my wife inside when you can. I'm going to work," Peter said. Wanhope nodded; she never spoke to him. Wanhope squeezed Verity's hand.

Peter left them on the porch. Away from the porch, he was called Doctor Ailey. Away from the porch, he had some dignity. Away from the porch, the air was not always thick with history. His wife. Her caretaker. Both stank of the smashed iron of that damn train. Of the river on fire. Of the blood and scars raised high like mountains over the whole body. Of the swollen red stump where once a delicate hand had skirted his skin to goosebumps. He was lucky she had remained mostly beautiful to the eyes; he had seen the rudimentary horrors of war, doughboys with faces sewn back together with other faces. She only had a missing hand, which he had advised her to keep hidden for the sake of the children, and a shiny, purple scar that ran from her hip socket to the outer edge of her knee. It crawled up her leg, hideous, and threatened to bite and poison him. It was venomous; so was the woman up the road from him. Who had been growing, summer by summer, from little Sistie to a woman, before he could recognize it. Penelope eyed him from her spot on the sidewalk.

He would greet her in a friendly manner on the road and head to Miller Duncan's place for a ride into the city. He would go to the white part of the mental hospital first, spending the day as an alienist examining and prescribing and keeping them calm and trying to tell the hospital director that malaria therapy would work on the syphilitic old man. Then he would go to the Black ward. Despite the controversy about cross-contamination and giving whites the Negroes' diseases, he would go to them, too. He believed in equality. He might say hello to a man from the Bramble Patch named Danuel, who'd moved to the city so that he could visit his son in the ward. He liked Danuel's kind manner. Peter would consider sterilization for a few patients, but only the really bad ones. He might suggest one to his surgeon. All the while, though, he would be thinking of Penelope's venomous body against his, knowing that the time would come that he would get bit. He walked past the house of Lazarus's benefactor.

What Laz liked most about the Hungarian Rhapsody was the way it held sorrow and transitioned effortlessly to caprice, as though sadness was a jacket you could shed when it got too warm. Ma Lyons had said: "You never shed your jacket in a white man's house. You cannot take off that jacket or else they'll think you were born without any sort of bringing up." Laz pressed his fingers into the minor key. The benefactor's second daughter, the brunette one with bright eyes, placed her head against the floorboards and felt the vibrations against her ears. He paused, feeling a swell in his knuckles, and she perked up and frowned. "Aimee, I can't no more," he said, and she nodded.

From the other parlor, her Pentecostal mother Mrs. Dorothée Keith looked on with her trembling hand gripping a cup of coffee. The cup shook violently as she watched Aimee run over to the Negro and sit next to him on the piano bench. Between her husband's delight in the boy and her daughter's growing affection, she feared the beast would snap and eat the whole household. Her husband had said: "Dolly, he's college-bound. We're helping to take him out of the brambles and mud and make him a real man. I doubt Reverend Kincaid's wife would have approached us if she thought he could be dangerous." This was not how he had said it, but she was too irritated to remember the exact words now as she sipped her coffee. She hated how he petted her head and called her Dolly, as if Dorothée was too difficult for his boorish mouth. She hated the Negro boy who played piano at that swamp place her preacher had warned her about. She hated that all their friends and family were being tricked into seeing the boy play music tonight and would be tricked into giving him money for "college." Mostly she hated that her husband was raising their kids Baptist instead of Pentecostal. She watched Lazarus and waited for his wild sensibilities to pounce on her little girl. He cracked his knuckles and began working on the Moonlight Sonata.

When he was at home last night, he had practiced Moonlight Sonata for his family, which was large and always growing. His eldest sister had four kids now, herself. They were good kids and sat still the whole time he played the piano. He noticed his little adopted sister sitting in the old rat traps, staring at a tintype. Then he played something more lively to cheer her up. Swanhilda's Waltz. She didn't look up. She was about to play her game. Wanhope's second-favorite game was sitting among the rat traps listening to Laz play the piano and looking at the tintype. The piano stank of the white man's house, a smell that every domestic in the Bramble Patch knew. One that irritated the nose. A smell that clung to most all of the women and girls in the Lyons house. Her mother hadn't had that smell. That much she remembered: an earthy smell that was silken against the nose. Her mother's photograph with eyes too bright and focused, "half-nekked" as Dinah would say, and happy. Wanhope remembered that she held tender sadness in those eyes. She would then begin the game: go up to Daddy King and say, "Daddy King, who's this?" The picture was the beginning of her favorite semiological discourse. She asked not because she did not know, but because the conversation would always conclude with *her* mother. One of the few things in the world that was hers only.

Verity clutched Wanhope's elbow and dug her claws into her brown flesh. "Stop."

Wanhope looked up from Ovid. Her throat burned with a mix of kerosene lamps and overtalking.

"The children are away?"

Wanhope nodded.

"And my husband telephoned and 's'not coming home for supper." She rose and touched Wanhope with the red stump where a hand had been. She rubbed her cheek delicately and Wanhope leaned into the touch, knowing that she would go home that night reeking of a white man's house. "Take me to the bath, then."

NOCTURNE

This is what the people said: "The Barghest's spent. His place. It's old-fashioned. No grind, no hump. No sex, you know. Where you going to slow drag and hully-gully? Shit, he got two dead whores now. Go into the marshes at Tempess's place. She has a good ear for music and good taste in liquor. Go listen to Lazarus play the piano. He's the best of us all."

The benefactor's older daughter, Marie-Anne, the one from the door, burst into the parlor with her plain white ballet dress and bare feet, which smacked against the floor. Lazarus hated that noise. She, too, was brunette, but unlike her sister, she was nearly diaphanous. She took a bow.

For the first time, girls her age were wearing painted lips and eyes lined in kohl. That was in the cities. That was where she would be a barnstormer in her dreams as she listened to the Hungarian Rhapsody. She danced upon the wood of her floor, standing in first position and second and third, doing a pirouette to the sounds of a Negro playing piano in her parlor. What her father didn't know was that these moments were as sacred as the last shafts of moonlight dancing up on the rooftop and more sacred than the tongues and utterances that she had heard her Pentecostal mother pray in. Her neck arched into an elegant bow, and she lifted her ears up through a line from the small of her back. A boy named Lazarus played the piano. And he was very good at it for somebody whose father picked peaches and grapes for a living.

Her little sister, Aimee, was almost deaf and watched the scene with ears pressed against the floorboards, following the rhythm that Lazarus tapped out with his feet. The little deaf girl looked at Marie-Anne and smiled so broadly that her cheeks threatened to rip in bloody gashes. Aimee could feel the music buried deep in her rib cage and rattling her bones, ready to spill them out in a game of craps. Since Lazarus, her father was letting her dance in the parlor or sit with company, when before she had to sit in the kitchen. Since Lazarus, her own world burst with drawings of amaryllis done in pastel chalk, made from the music he made with the piano. She would say to Lazarus, play something for Marie-Anne to dance to. And he would answer her back and play the music. He would not stare coldly at her lips as she spoke, nor wrinkle his nose, but would actually listen to her.

Lazarus played his way through the overture of *Coppelia*, almost dreaming that he sat in front of an orchestra and watched a prima perform *soubresauts* to the ballet of his fingers. In the dream, he wears a white tailcoat which he removes in a swoop, because the stage is his stage. In the dream, he hunches over the keys and begins a waltz. But then he switches mid-waltz to his favorite blues, and the people scream for him. Up in the balcony, Ma Lyons is smiling in a fine fox fur, the kind Mrs. Dorothée had in the closet. Dinah's in a silk dress instead of cotton so old that sweat has turned the collar to rags. Daddy King is telling the white man next to him that he's Laz's daddy. Bessie is holding his baby in the front row, bouncing him to the rhythm. The prima is doing a *grand jeté*. Bessie's brother Tommy is playing fiddle right next to him, because that's what they do when they play the hully-gully.

But it seemed that Esther wasn't in this half-dream. She was at the river, pulling up the mud and rocks and flogging herself bloody with them. She was in the sulfur plains, where music could soothe no longer.

Three things that happened back in 1915 catalyzed 1920: Lazarus asked his friend Tommy from down the road if he could fiddle with him at Tempess's place, and they learned a version of "Alexander's Ragtime Band" that swept up everyone in fervor; soon, the Barghest noticed people weren't showing up to his place no more. The second was what happened to Dr. Peter Ailey's first daughter, Geraldine, just over the age of one. Verity was holding her tightly in the crook of her bad arm, and the child dropped and fell swiftly toward the ground. Luckily, Verity's own mother was there helping her and cradled the little girl before she could smash her head upon the teakwood. Verity begged her mother not to tell her husband. But Peter knew even before he got home what had occurred. He raged against his wife's stump arm, beating his belt into the air where a hand had been. "Of course you thought you could carry that child. What if Geraldine had broken her skull? What would you have done then?" (He was in medical school at the time and loved using his knowledge of anatomy to shame her.) The last thing was that D. W. Griffith made a horror film of real nightmares that set Mrs. Dorothèe Keith's teeth on edge. Her littlest, Aimee, was a toddler yet, small and bright and going deaf, and her husband had invited a Negro boy into the home. She watched Lillian Gish fall down to the craggy surface below and screamed in the theater. A few women did. *The New York Globe* called it "the greatest picture ever made and the greatest drama ever filmed." Dorothèe felt that in her stomach. Like a sucker punch.

THESE BONES

Five years later, thinking back on when she watched *Birth of a Nation*, Dorothèe sneered at Lazarus. "Boy. My husband wants to know what you want for supper," she said.

"I'll eat anything, Mrs. Dorothèe. Is Mr. Richard going to be home soon? I don't want to bother you with my practice."

"Don't you mind me with your practicing. My husband and me have investment on you doing well. So you keep practicing. All day if you have to." She hissed at her oldest daughter to come help her in the kitchen. She watched the boy and thought of that movie.

Down the road, Geraldine Ailey's shrill cry was echoing through the whole house. Verity grabbed her arm to stop her from running but Geraldine, now six, wrenched away, her blonde halo of hair flying behind her. Her younger sister Sally, aged three, was swinging a porcelain doll by the roots of its hair. The baby doll's head cracked against the highboy. Sally was stark naked and joyously jumping.

"Damn Black girl. Ain't here to help me!"

Wanhope was dreaming in the barn loft up with the barn kittens. Her jaw dropped and crude oil spilled from her mouth, dripping from her sanguine tongue. She felt the color build behind her eyes lavender and gold and navy. Oil pooled onto the straw. Her toenails dug into the wool of her stockings. The kittens scattered, save the gray tabby boy. Then she exploded—her body flew in all directions, a rainbow of crude oils spilled from her severed self. By the time Wanhope put her body back together, the sun had dipped behind the Aileys' oak tree. She scooped up her kitten and placed him in her apron pocket. She ran into the Aileys' house, coated in sweat and the smell of dinner.

"I gave you permission to get some dinner. Not to leave forever. I need you!"

"I'm sorry."

"Will you give the babies some of my headache powder to cool them down? Send them to bed without eating." The little one began licking the side of a sliver of porcelain. "Help me curl my hair for tonight. I want it in ringlets. Fifty-four of them. Do you understand?"

Wanhope grabbed the littlest one from her spot where she was stroking shards of doll face.

"Elizabeth."

Wanhope jumped at the sound of her middle name.

"Thank you for helping me with Sally and Deenie today. When I leave for the concert, you may go home for the night."

Mr. Richard was smashing potatoes between his teeth the way apes did, with particular attention to the fibrous skins between each grind of his jaw. The way Mr. Richard could masticate and talk so eloquently was proof to Lazarus that whiteness was so much different than Blackness. He was able to construct a world in which he would be so rich and elegant that the thought of eating and talking at once would not disgust him. His hands ached at the red band that was his knuckles. He heard Mr. Richard say something about playing "Alexander's Ragtime Band," which was Mr. Richard's favorite song. He often requested it. Sometimes, he would even allow Lazarus to bring his friend Tommy to fiddle with him. Not tonight. There was a local white violinist, Mr. Richard had noted, that would be playing with him. "Good man. One of the Croswells."

Lazarus tried to lift his fork and found himself all-overish. The tremor started in his legs and raced up to his right hand. Mrs. Dorothée looked at him, eyes brimmed with tears. The fork clattered onto the china, chipping a little piece away from the Delftware blue. "It's just nerves," he said. "I just can't eat too well." Mr. Richard nodded. Marie-Anne giggled. Mrs. Dorothée clenched her fork tighter.

Sometimes Lazarus wondered if it might be all right for him to tell Mr. Richard more about himself. Laz hadn't told his own father that his girlfriend was pregnant, but she was. And sometimes Laz imagined that he could sit with Mr. Richard on the nice couch in the nice parlor and talk about it. Mr. Richard would hand him a cigar and offer him a glass of red wine. Mr. Richard would place his hand on his shoulder, and Laz would ask: "What's it even mean to be a father, Mr. Richard? Daddy King's always too busy with working for Mr. Duncan and with all them damn children, sorry for the language, but they are damned." They were eight in total; some born to his parents and some not, and that didn't include the kids that Dinah had. And that didn't include the town that looked up to Daddy King. He had a lot of children that way too. Mr. Richard gave his daughters a small forehead kiss good night, every night. No one was more loved in the world than they.

Lazarus dug his fork into the roast beef; the hair on the back of his neck prickled. He could barely lift his hand to his mouth.

Mr. Richard was talking too much about the white folk in Napoleonville and the money and the Negro College and how Lazarus would get out of the Bramble Patch. As if the Bramble Patch was something you could tangle your way out of. As if Mercy City didn't run in your veins, or you could wean yourself from Tempess's liquor. As if you were not scarred in the legs from getting switched by the white sheriff while going back home. As if you could ever take off your jacket in a white man's house. Or as if the knot in your stomach—the one sloshing the bile around like your little brother sloshes a bucket of pig slop—was not every warning bell that you knew from the trains that passed through. As if you could ever leave the Bramble Patch. As if you could even try.

COMPLINE

The Barghest had watched the world for over sixty years. He felt the pickling in his stomach turning him inside out. He remembered the Brick-man and Jessup, and 'Livia when she still had the O. His ribs threatened to lacerate his skin for their own pleasure. He liked pleasure, and silk and habanera dances and girly shows and the fresh blood of men. Shit, he loved it all. Where Mercer Street began, a little ways off from Freedom Road, he had slithered his way into the last crooked building on the wooden sidewalk. That was 1890. Now it was 1920. He had seen wars of a sort sprinkle the land with fresh droplets of blood and virility. He watched white men of note sneak into his shows; the preacher and his son made him laugh because they never saw each other, only the same woman. He had seen the last rag hands start to dwindle and had seen them begin. He knew bump. He knew grind. He missed both. Tempess had a good piano man who was young and had quick hands. She had no dead whore on her back, hunching her shoulders. She had no taste for flesh. She was not starving.

But had he waited a little longer, Tempess would've been without a piano man and soon without a fiddler, so she'd have dried up. The making of liquor would have dried her up, too, when the sheriff caught wind of it. Had he waited, a Depression would have socked her in the mouth straight, blunt force-like, and she would have hemorrhaged money until she drowned, and the river would surge up and down everywhere her and her family, Bertha's people, lived, and would swallow up everything she owned.

The Barghest turned his nose up the hill to where the white folk lived. He smelled something...alone. Something unfettered to life, a pure piece of flesh, so sad. So very, very sad. Hollowed-soul, soured-soul blood. That was his favorite kind of blood. And so the Barghest stepped out of the what-if and followed the sugary delight of blood bathed in the pallor of the nearly new moon.

Could you picture him? Lazarus, coming forth onto the stage of a school auditorium, at the shoreline of an unending sea of faces so unlike his own they seem to be masks? Faces he recognizes but does not give names to other than sir or ma'am? Ready to tear down the black and white keys with scampering fingers, blessed hands arched and hovering, his shoulders in a hunch?

Lazarus felt the blood leave his hands. He was cold. The air sucked from his lungs. He looked at the notes on the page, looked at his violinist but could not put a name to his face.

Or could you picture him the way he has been engrained into little Aimee's mind as she sits on her mother's lap? Vertebrae jutting out into menacing little humps, fingers snapping the spine of his song book to a page where the inky darkness of the notes cavorts into the rests, small eyes against the blackest skin she would ever know darting to pick each of them apart? Her mother vibrated in pain. She would remember it, the tremor that ran across her hippocampus, seventeen years later, when she would return to Napoleonville, camera at her side, to capture justice. She would say to her sister Marie-Anne and to Deena, who grew up down the street, that she remembered her mother had been afraid of Lazarus. They would barely understand her.

"Who was Alexander to have a ragtime band?" Tommy Teller would one day say in an interview with Alan Lomax. "He wasn't nobody for which the music could be named. Irving Berlin, he's Russian Jew. He didn't make that music. But folk think he did. 'Specially where I'm from. I hate that song. It soured my soul."

The Croswell with the violin tapped his feet to lead in the music. For a moment, the black and white keys blurred into an image of gray from which the chromatic scale might appear in brilliant shades of the blues. Any minute now. Any minute now. The Croswell with the violin tapped his feet again, but Lazarus, he was stuck where his knucklebones had frozen in searing pain. Mr. Richard's eyes grew huge—tall, like Wanhope would say. His mouth opened and his whiskers drooped.

"I'm sorry, ladies and gentlemen. If you would be patient, I—" Lazarus stopped short as he heard his own voice. He what? Felt ill suddenly? Couldn't play the piano anymore? Had a child on the way? Wanted to go to college so he and Bessie could get married and get out of the Bramble Patch? Believed that there was a place beyond the Bramble Patch for him to go in the first place?

He bolted from the piano bench.

Lazarus leaned against the outside wall breathing in shuddering heaves. He watched his hands shake and redden. He bit into his thumb, hoping to wrench it back awake, but he only drew blood.

"What are you doing?"

Mr. Richard gripped Laz's collar by the front so his neck bulged over the fabric and he started to choke a little. "Mr. Richard, sir, please."

The grip loosened a little. Laz opened his mouth and said his hands were run ragged and he needed a break for a week. He wouldn't play at Tempess's or anything, he just needed to pause. A few days. He was feeling ill in his stomach and his head and his hands and his mind. His hands were the worst of all. Hand-sick is what he called it. He was hand-sick. Mr. Richard would understand. Mr. Richard would know, because he was a good father, that Lazarus needed rest. Mr. Richard would—

SMACK!

Right into the ear. Blood began to pool near Laz's auricle. He staggered back against the wall, and the ringing, God, the ringing, which sounded like the tin music box Marie-Anne played for him. The song it played was the Für Elise. Every night he was at the Keiths' house, he would play it for the girls as a lullaby. Aimee would place her ear to the floor and Marie-Anne would sit cross-legged and play the music box to accompany him. Sometimes, he played so softly that they could hear the gear churn inside the machine. He wished Tommy was here to help him stand up straight, because he was halfway slipped down the wall. He wished

THESE BONES

Tommy could get his Grandma Ady to make up one of her horse-chestnut teas to help soothe his whole body. He thought about Bessie hugging him tightly as he scrambled to his feet. He was tear-blind; Mr. Richard had turned into a nighttime mirage. In the haze, he experienced the man vaguely. Go home. They would talk in the morning. If he was sick, go home.

The blood pooled in his ears made him half-deaf. He gripped his knees and inched his way down Main Street. He slunk into the shadows of the cool of the moon. He remembered being young, watching Esther do this, her saying she was turning into tar. He thought of the tar people she said lined the street these days, faces shrouded in the stickiness, and they reached out from their existence into his own. He had used to believe Esther, but he was nearly eighteen now. There was no time for Esther's odd words, half-past and future tenses. Bessie and the baby who was coming and college. That was all he had. And maybe his body had rejected his hands because college was not his either. That would be okay. His whole life he'd heard about Br'er Rabbit stories and got familiar with growing up in thorny places. It makes you clever, perhaps wise enough to stay put. They'd build a life: Bessie and him and the baby. He was the son of a peach picker and a seamstress, and of this patch of earth, twisted up and thorny. There, from the corner of his tear-stained eyes, he caught a glimpse of the hunched figure of the Barghest, gnawing on fifty-four ringlet curls.

Fifty-four blonde curls were scrunched in the bloody hands of the Barghest, who crouched a few feet from what was once Verity Ailey's head. The moon lit up his blueish skin as he bent down and licked her sweet blood from the mud. Having taken only poor, black, dusty blood, he found this decadent blood near royal in his mind—like a fine wine pressed in the light of the nearly new moon, and just as intoxicating—thick with delight. He wanted more with each bite of her body, pure and hollow. It smeared his lips. It dripped onto his tongue. It ate him back in a sweetness that burned his esophageal lining. It choked him a little, soldering one side of his throat to the other. She was good.

The scalp and strands would be haphazardly sewn back on her head and the fifty-four blonde curls would remain youthful until their decay. A diadem of roses would be placed to hide the jagged stitch line. Her mother's beautification club friends would sit in the back of the Second Baptist Church and talk from underneath their hats.

"She looks good," one will say. "That Dickens man did a good job with her."

"You probably couldn't tell that she was murdered if you didn't know already," the other will reply. The mortician will even have stuffed her ribcage full of cotton fluff to keep her body from collapsing. It will seem a marvel.

The Barghest looked up to Lazarus, eyes beady and satisfied. He held his finger to his lips to shush the boy. Lazarus looked up to the end of the street. His voice moved before his brain could stopper it up. So, it spilled into the night. On Main Street in Napoleonville, not down Freedom Road in the Bramble Patch. Once, when he was a child, he had attempted to pick up an armful of peaches only to watch them drop and bruise and litter the entire floor; some snuck out the door into the wild street. His voice scattered and rolled away like that escaped fruit in Marion Chapman's store.

He caught a glimpse of the Barghest shimmering into the darkness and ran to the body, ran into the pool of blood knees-first. He cradled the scalp and tried to stitch it back to the head using only his mind. He saw her face, serene and quiet. He had passed her on the porch, seen her with his adopted sister brushing her hair or holding her babies. Once she'd offered him a glass of water on a hot day and one other time, she had him chop some wood for her in the back. She had talked about a horse in the field where there wasn't one; she spoke of her husband's affair with a neighbor. She was sad, always sad, always half gone. His sister would carry that curdled sadness home to her little nest among the rat traps.

"Mrs. Verity?" he whispered. Spittle drained from his mouth on to her eyes. He was crying, dropping tears onto her crepe dress and into her hair now as he leaned to listen for any sign of life. "Mrs. Verity? Please. Please. God. Please."

He took off his jacket to stopper the blood. He knew Ma Lyons would be furious at it, but he could not help but try to stopper the blood. It did nothing but soak the jacket further; he began to cry harder and watched the shadows of the moon dance across her little nose and lacquered mouth. She had near a smile in the red of her own blood. She was pale blue. He was dark blue. He had to get help, but he could not bring himself to leave this poor woman alone in the dark when the Barghest might come back to pick her apart. He looked up and framed the stars while he prayed that God would send help. He caressed her bloodied cheek with his swollen knuckles and looked down on the pale blue face.

The light changed. His shadow covered her face, which was now white and red with death and blood. The ringing in his ear gave way to a growl. He knew that growl came from a Dodge, Mr. Richard's Dodge. He felt snot drip down his shirt, not daring to gaze into the light but letting it bathe the back of his head.

"Dolly. Tell the girls to look away."

"Richard. I told you! I told you!"

"Dorothée. Enough."

"Look what he did! You let him in our home! You let him near our girls!"

"Take the car! Go home!"

Footsteps crunched on the dirt road. Daddy King said that someday this street would look like the streets in the city, plastered over in stone. Daddy King seemed to know a lot. Lazarus wanted to ask him how to be a father now, too. Was this what it was like, holding a scalped woman back together again? He clutched her shoulders and tried to find the words: "It was the Barghest." He screamed that in his mind over and over. But his mouth just spittled into pools around her head. Her eyes looked violet by moonlight and headlight. A second car engine roared.

"Peter, don't come down here!"

"Is that her?"

"*Peter.*" That was Mr. Richard's threat voice.

"What'd that black bastard do to my wife!"

Claws dug into Laz's shoulders and wrenched him backward into the mud. He let go of Mrs. Verity's head. Her scalp went into the air. That was all he saw as he covered his face from the incoming blows.

"Son of a bitch!" Dr. Peter said. "Son of a bitch! Nigger shit! Son of a bitch!"

He flailed his hands against Laz's body, finding every point he could to make the pain grow. Laz heard a crack in his ribcage, and the pain burned through his body. Fists came down on his ears; the ringing got worse. This time not a music-box ringing but the sound of when you find yourself drowning. Laz felt pain in this calf, right where his switchback of scars was. Again. They blistered anew and opened up. All the keloid tissue began to ooze rivers of Lazarus onto the back of his pants. For a moment, he thought that his pants might be ruined. But as he felt his body tremble, he knew he might not have to worry about his clothes anymore.

A knife slid down his spine, opening up his shirt and epidermis, opening little strings of fat and exposing them to Dr. Peter's blows. Lazarus was slowly being transformed into a delta of blood. More hands were on him than before. Nails dug into his scalp as a voice shrieked. Rivulets came down into his eyes and God, they stung. Worse than that bee on his lip this morning. The blood got into his crying mouth, and he could only choke on himself.

Then he felt the blows hush. A hand grabbed his, gently. He had learned his lesson—don't take off your jacket in a white man's house, he thought over and over, don't go anywhere that don't lead back to alive. The hand traced his own delicately as if his fingers were frail slivers of glass upon which one might cut the skin. Fingers encircled his thumb, a thumb braced against his where the proximal phalanx and the metacarpal met. Lazarus would not have known this, but Peter Ailey did. He knew how to wrench the thumb back with his finger and push back the joint with his thumb. He knew to do it slowly so that the son of a bitch would scream in fear first and then in pain second. He looked over his wife's corpse as he did it. He saw her mangled and nested hair so far strewn from her head; her crepe de chine dress disheveled; her snake-like scar exposed for the world to see; her hand, lost seven years prior, which had once had fingers that intertwined with his. He heard the *pop* of the joint snapping and breathed a sigh of relief.

Lazarus cried out as he felt Mr. Richard's knife touch the flesh of his thumb, dig in, slice, fillet it. His piano, his hully-gully, his valse, his ragtime, his rhapsody all disappeared as the flesh hung from the bone. That is what made him keen as several pairs of hands lifted him up and carried him towards the white side of town. His voice spilled out; this time, though, it spilled out towards the Bramble Patch.

Tommy gripped Bessie's hand. Through the years of her life, through all that she would think of her brother after he left, she would always come back to this moment: when he held her hand so tight as they fled into the night. When she'd tell her son, Lyman, about the night his daddy died, she'd say: "Your uncle Tommy hasn't done everything right, but that night he did not let me go."

Tommy had held his breath in the plunge into the night, when he heard Ma Lyons scream into the street and up and down the river. It was an echo of her son's scream; she had heard it from the town above in the Patch below. Lazarus screamed and her house rattled; the world herself shook and Ma amplified the sound. One day, when he would record in a studio, Tommy would look at the microphone and remember how the one scream had amplified the other. Tonight, he grabbed his sister's hand and pulled her through the Bramble Patch.

"White folks took him," he said. "There's a rumor going round that he killed Mrs. Ailey and ate her."

Bessie shook her head as they skirted the river, where Esther rocked back and forth in prayer, throwing dust upon her face and neck. By the waters of Babylon, thought Bessie, we wept as we remembered Zion. She could not contain her tears the way the river could not contain all the sadness of the world. Esther was the embodiment of sackcloth and ashes all rolled into one. Bessie stopped for a moment. And she watched Esther bathe herself in dirt and soot. She memorized the alignment of the heavens that night and saw the particles of dust fall from moonbeams onto Esther's breasts and settle there.

"How can we sing the Lord's song in a foreign land?" her future husband would preach one day. As a deacon in the AME, he'd be giving the pastor a break, ten years later in 1930—the same year the flood would come. Her six-year-old, Luella, and her son, Lyman, would flank her in the pew. And while the whole congregation would think the foreign land was this earthly plane and home was Beulahland, Bessie knew that home could become foreign and strange in an instant.

Bessie would be the last person to weep when the flood came in the summer of 1930, because long ago, so much of her hope had drowned anyway; it was in this moment, watching Esther at the river.

Esther and Tommy moved into the coolness of the trees. Knowing that if they came too close to the road, they might get swept up in the anger.

Someone said that some white folk had come down to the junction where Marion's store was and had busted the windows. They were coming for the Bramble Patch and would set brushfire to it if they had to.

"He didn't do it, Tommy."

"I know." Every man in the Bramble Patch had a hunch as to who it was. No one could ever name the fear.

THESE BONES

They whispered between the trees, scuffing up pine needles as they went. Listless wind encircled them in the dark, and hovering over it all was the moon.

When Tommy was in his fifties, high as high could go, he told his second wife the story of watching the moon settle above Napoleonville. How she crept up and smiled a big old broad grin when Bessie and Tommy broke through the clearing. "Bessie wouldn't go no further. She didn't want to see him. She didn't want to be seen."

In the tall grass, they slumped into the mud and watched the moon. They could hear his screaming. They weren't far. Bessie jammed her palms over her ears. "No more," she whispered. "No more."

Tommy draped his arm over his sister's shoulder. He listened. He listened to cries of agony turn to gurgles and then grow too dim to hear. His cheeks grew slightly warmer, but he pretended they did not. The moon was suddenly shrouded in a blue haze that dampened the light. Through the trees a dim glow could be seen, but he pretended it could not. He looked at Bessie, who looked up where the moon had been. Strung-out Tommy in his fifties, resting his head on his wife's bosom in his stupor, could still see her silhouette.

"Tommy?" asked Bessie.

"Mhm."

"Are those clouds or smoke?" asked Bessie.

They were too quiet. And then he said, "What's bad is I can't tell you."

REQUIEM

Hell is the end of a rope where the arthritis-twisted hand of Marion Chapman fumbles with a dull blade—watching him cut down your sweetheart.

Hell is the old man rubbing your belly. The water poisoned by your lover's blood. Hell is having the whole town quench their thirst with his blood. And his empty casket, placed into a hole in the woods. What was left of his body had been tossed into the river by the sheriff and was later found scuttled on Tata and Rhea's island. His putrified abdomen burst suddenly at midday, spattering the edenic sunflower patch and the baby's bassinette. Auntie Rhea found Snow-baby gored up. Tata Duende knew from his circus days that he could sell the body as an oddity. And so he did. Peter Ailey bought the body. Taxidermied it. This is Hell.

Hell is the Barghest growing pregnant with his own delight at everyone's suffering, especially Tempess's. Hell is seeing your lover's hands butchered so skillfully into thin slices that it could have been done in a delicatessen. In Harlem, they hung the black and white flag for him: "A man was lynched today." But that's Harlem. This is the Bramble Patch. This is Hell.

Hell is a breech birth for one of the dead man's twin sons. So he comes out strangled like his father before him. His uncle takes him away, so you won't see. But you do—you see the blue of his lips and his knuckles. He has his father's nose.

And his living brother cries, and you flip him towards your breast for him to suckle, but your chapped nipples burn and bleed instead. It will be Marion Chapman's tangled fingers resting on your cheek as he asks for your hand in marriage. You say yes, inasmuch as you have any say. Soon the new year comes: 1921, the first year the world has no Lazarus Lyons. Some white man goes door to door selling photos of your lover's death to curious white folk. The Barghest's place gets a better piano man and gets busy again. He likes white blood. So sweet. This is Hell.

Bessie Teller Chapman was the Queen of Hell.

FROM *HEARTLAND MELODIES: INSPIRATIONS FOR BLUES STANDARDS FROM MIDDLE AMERICA*

Chicago's Tommy "Bobwhite" Teller is a perfect example of a writer whose work has location-specific historicity as well as universal appeal. Teller's song "Flame-licked Lover", for example, references the famous Chicago fire of 1871 throughout but simultaneously describes an affair between unfaithful lovers. As Teller's biographer Markus Kennedy notes:

> His contemporaries anthologized this song in particular, because its symbolism seemed to resonate everywhere and with everyone.

Bassist Freddy Lipton, who played with Teller between 1944 and 1958, said it was a particular favorite of his: "I ain't ever known that song to not work a crowd. We played everywhere from London to San Francisco, and 'Flame-licked Lover' always got people cheering. I bet it's the only time Mrs. O'Leary's cow got applause." The lyrics capture the universal experience of jealously while remaining a pure Chicago classic.[1]

Some lyrics in Teller's work have the opposite effect, becoming almost hauntingly personal in their lack of specificity, as in the early recording from 1931, "Don't Lead Back to Alive." The work is markedly primitive; Teller still features the fiddle as his lead instrument instead of his signature guitar, yet Kennedy calls these lyrics "achingly personal" despite the lack of reference to a particular location: "The moon was shrouded in blue fog/ and it was hard for her to tell/ if clouds were what the pines were showered in/ or the smoky cracklings of Negro skin."

---

[1] Markus Kennedy, *Mournful Hollerin': The Life and Music of Tommy 'Bobwhite' Teller* (Chicago, IL: Easterly Winds Press, 1999).

THESE BONES

Rev. Jonah Kincaid of Napoleonville Second Baptist

Lord, bless me and my flock! Give me Your words. Soften the hearts of my flock, Lord, Abba Father. Give them ears to hear me. Bury their sinful nature, Lord. Strangle it. Strangle them with Your wrath as they give in to their temptations. My flock is a weak and idle people in a weak and idle age. Help them, Father. Amen and amen.

Brothers and Sisters. I will be reading from the Book of Exodus, chapter 32, verses 19 through 25. "And it came to pass, as soon as he came nigh unto the camp, that he saw the calf, and the dancing: and Moses' anger waxed hot, and he cast the tables out of his hands, and brake them beneath the mount. And he took the calf which they had made, and burnt it in the fire, and ground it to powder, and strewed it upon the water, and made the children of Israel drink of it. And Moses said unto Aaron, What did this people unto thee, that thou hast brought so great a sin upon them? And Aaron said, Let not the anger of my lord wax hot: thou knowest the people, that they are set on mischief. For they said unto me, Make us gods, which shall go before us: for as for this Moses, the man that brought us up out of the land of Egypt, we wot not what is become of him. And I said unto them, Whosoever hath any gold, let them break it off. So they gave it me: then I cast it into the fire, and there came out this calf. And when Moses saw that the people were naked (for Aaron had made them naked unto their shame among their enemies); then Moses stood in the gate of the camp, and said, Who is on the Lord's side? let him come unto me. And all the sons of Levi gathered themselves together unto him."

This has been the word of the Lord.

My flock, many'll tell you that this is an epoch of progress, of automobiles and aeroplanes, of full bellies and radios. I mean, MY voice, this voice, this instrument of God, can be heard anywhere in the county. Outside of Napoleonville, there are those who can hear me. They'll tell you.

But, there ain't been a righteous generation in a long, long time. We all know what sort of vice can come from drunkenness. First it's a glass with your friends, then a couple of glasses to keep you warm at night, soon you're kicking up a rumpus, soon after impoverished of body, spirit, and wallet, then those friends you were chummy with desert you, soon you take to crime to keep up that fast lifestyle, soon you're in the grave, yessir, my flock, leaving behind your women and children defenseless in the cold air. All 'cause you are of this wicked and depraved age and not the kingdom of God.

I've seen you. I've seen you all, walking down Mercer Street like it in't the mouth of Hell, like the whores of Babylon, those daughters of Ham, aren't enticing you with their songs of vice and delight. They call it Mercy City down there, my flock. I know it, I know it well.

That's an irony, for there is no mercy for those who fraternize with prostitution, drunkenness, and miscegenation. Yes, wives, your husbands go down to the Bramble Patch and sleep with the Negresses with their own money, the money reserved for their families, listening to that hot music. Not even music. That noise that is banged out on the piano and blasted out of coronets near every night.

You are part of this weak and idle generation, men and women who fall into sin by falling into unlawful practices. I've seen you in your hushed, dark minds crying "Hosanna! Save us," crying for help as you guzzle whiskey off the bare breasts of Ham's daughters, as you lick up froth across her collarbone and suckle dregs from her nipples. I hate to be indelicate for the ewes of my flock, but the rams of my flock know what they have done. What of our Negro brothers and sisters, you may ask? Well, we surely can't expect them to be as moral as we are, my flock. We just can't. My wife, Eugenia—stand up, Eugenia darling. Isn't she just God's gift? Eugenia, here, took the time to do a survey of the townsfolk and their history. Perhaps you've seen it on display at the library. What was it you found out about the Bramble Patch, there, honey? What's that? You're gonna have to speak up for my flock to hear you. That's right, the Negroes basically stole that land there from the Missus's family years back. Thank you. Sit down, honey. You all know that they are just not able to maintain that same level of morality as us whites, now. We expect nothing more from the Negro; they don't have the intellectual capacity to comprehend and maintain the standards of conduct set forth for us in the Bible. Why, how many of the Negroes in the Bramble Patch do you think have read the Bible? How many of them do you think can even read?

But you? You wicked souls condemned to fiery pits but saved by the blood of Christ? You have read the scriptures for yourselves and have tested and approved the will of the Father. And now you sicken Him with your drinking and fraternizing. Jesus called the white man to this continent to create a beautiful covenant with Him, to carve out a nation for His glory and honor. And you now crawl into those dens of iniquity like cockroaches.

And that's what the Lord sees when he sees you: cock-roaches in the brothels.

You see, Moses, when he was speaking with God, was told that something was mighty wrong, and when he went down the mountain, he saw the people were worshipping a golden calf without any regard for their own salvation. I said without a *single* regard for their salvation. See, they were, like us, part of a depraved epoch. Some of them didn't know any better. They had been in Africa, amongst a morally inferior people, worshipping golden idols with orgies and songs like you do today, only your idols are booze and the daughters of Ham. Amen? Amen. But who are you in the story? Who represents you, my brothers and sisters? Why, it is Aaron, Aaron the brother of Moses, who had stood as witness and who was called the highest priest. He is you and you are he. Because Aaron knew better. He knew better than to cast the gold into a false god, because he had seen a true one. Yes, knew Him personally. Like I know my wife, Eugenia. Like I know that she uses rose water for perfume. Like I know the secret ingredient in her maple sugar pies. Now, ladies, I'm a husband of honor, so I swore I wouldn't tell. But I do know the secret. Aaron knew God like I know my wife's ironing schedule. I know my wife, because I've seen my wife at work. If I chose to ignore all I know about that beautiful woman you see in front of you, because of people who don't know her, then I have failed. I have failed her. I would not be a good shepherd to my home if I let other people sway me into unrighteousness towards my wife.

See, that's what being a scofflaw is, flock. It is knowing what is the right way of living and turning your back on all of that. For what? For a few minutes of pleasure? Cause the Israelites sure made a big fuss about how great Aaron was when he gave them the calf, right? I bet Aaron felt pretty good about himself when they were chanting his name and calling him good. And I bet you feel good, too. You're drinking with gusto. You're dancing your worries away. You're enjoying a woman. It all feels so good.

Depart from that wickedness. Depart and do not tarry. Depart and do not look back. Depart and do not return, lest you be forsaken by the one we call Savior. Those sons and daughters of Ham cannot resist the devil. But we can. By God's grace, we can.

And now, Sister Paula will lead our choir in "Onward, Christian Soldiers." Thank you all.

MAID AND COOK: A DIALOGUE
1927

"I don't want to get in trouble."

"Who's gonna get you in trouble? They don't see us."

"Keep your voice down."

"They think we're dumb, deaf, and blind. That you *just* cook and I *just* clean and Ernest *just* buttles, or we are just dust gathering in the corner, waiting to be swept away. They don't see me with a trail of firefly light leaping from my footsteps as I walk down the road. How the sun turns my skin into gold. How the moon turns my skin into lapis."

"But still—"

"They don't hear my words wrapped in ermine and your songs stirred into a pot of greens. They don't know we hear them, either. And they don't know we talk about them behind their back. Cause they don't listen. Now tell me what happened."

"It was Wednesday, I think? When I went with the Missus to the church board meeting? I went up to go to the ladies' I saw Samuel Kincaid walk in late and say: 'It's time, Daddy! Time for me to take over the church.'"

"Wait! He didn't see you?"

"You sound angry."

"We are *nothing* to them."

"That's not entirely true."

"Maybe a hammer or a wash basin."

"More like a mule."

"Maybe a pair of hands. But nothing more than that."

"Point is Samuel Kincaid wants the church."

"It sours a soul."

"Why do you say that?"

"You see where his hands go on the Lyons girl?"

"On her dress?"

"On her ass."

"No worse than his father. Seen him buy a night or two on Mercy Street."

"Samuel's different. I seen him—"

"Hush, Missus is coming.… Afternoon, ma'am. I'm just helping her finish up the dishes.… Supper tonight? Well, I know how much we like a special Friday supper, so I prepared the chicken for roasting.… No ma'am, I… Are Mr. and Mrs. Chalmers bringing their boys, too?… I'll pick up the lamb soon as we're done with dishes. Thank you, ma'am."

"…"

"…"

"…"

"I hate to say it—"

"Say it anyway."

"That bitch! I am halfway through brining the chicken and she turn around and say, 'No, we're having the Chalmers over, so rack o' lamb.'"

"Shit. It's not even Easter or something fancy."

"You wanna know what the worst part is?"

"What?"

"She's gonna say the chicken's over-seasoned tomorrow."

"Sours a soul, honey! Air in this house is stale as a coffin. Hotter than one, too."

"You're right, though. They don't see us, do they?"

"Crows line the gables, the Missus's pillow made a death crown last night, shadows ooze down the wallpaper, and they don't see it. How they gonna see us?"

"What you mean by that?"

"I mean the wind is changing to things of sorrow. And they won't know it if it hit them."

"You're imagining things."

"Oh yeah? Well, how come I saw the white Reverend at the grave of Jessup doing 'business'? They don't see us, so they don't care if we see them."

"..."

"..."

"You're lying."

"You want me to be lying."

"You're lying."

"What I got to lie about? They're the ones with secrets. They're the ones who have things to hide."

"Don't—"

"We always stood in the sun and let the light kiss our skin with bronze and cocoa. Let our hair mop up the heat. Made the world turn when we swayed our hips. We don't need shadows. We don't need secrets."

"I know it's not right to hate, but I hate that man."

"Not as bad as his son."

"What his son do?"

"He got the witchy Lyons girl pregnant."

"I can't—that poor girl. She don't know up from down."

"But that ain't the worst of it, honey."

"No?"

"He takes her to one of them doctors to get it out. It works, but she got sick. Now she can't have babies."

"Miracle she lived."

"Mmm."

"What Ma Lyons say about it?"

"What you mean? He's the Reverend's son. And sounds to me, he'll be running them white folks someday."

"God!"

"Not like you to cuss the Lord."

"They *don't* see us, do they?"

"No. But I see you. You are phosphorescence against tide. The stunning heart of gold and black incased in a shroud of wonder. So we'll take care of own, now. Don't let them devour your light. That's what they want."

"…"

"…"

"Sours a soul, though, don't it?"

"Bit by bit, it does."

ANTEDILUVIAN

Marion Chapman is watching his son and Snow-baby and a couple of Dinah's kids play hopscotch in the dirt. This summer's hotter than usual in his estimation. He thinks it's 'cause Napoleonville is mostly paved roads now, even Freedom Road and Mercer and a couple of streets here in the Bramble Patch. Snow-baby's probably going to turn red in the sun. She looks white, and he knows folks are suspicious. But he's good friends with her papa and momma and knows she's genuine. His son isn't, really, but he loves him despite.

"Marion," says David, from the pickle barrel. "There's a nigra down in Henwen that says he bought one of those radios from the Sears."

"And?"

"He said he put it in his barber shop so that the men can come in and listen to stuff over the wireless."

"And?"

"I'm just saying. It's been a few years since they been on the market. A used one wouldn't be too expensive. Nigra's getting them from Sears new even."

"You know what's on that radio? White reverends. That jazz music. Bad news. We got all that here. Hell, the Reverend here in Napoleonville's on the radio anyway. I can get his shit for free."

Mr. Chapman looks at David and can recognize his own wrinkles and graying hair. David was a boy not so long ago, following his mother and father back and forth from the church to the funeral home. David smells of death, but Marion finds that comforting. His wife, so young, smells too much like spring. It disconcerts him.

"Yeah, but you know what, they got Tommy Teller on the wireless now. He's got some songs that get played."

Tommy Teller has always been a bit of a troublemaker. And even though he's now kin by marriage, he still irks Marion. What talent he has is almost certainly not as prominent as his vices.

The door opens and the Barghest walks in. His teeth are big. It's odd, because Marion had never noticed it until a few years ago, but now every time he sees him he thinks, "My, what big teeth he has." The Barghest is all smiles and pressed arrow collars. He has a lapel pin, by God, a lapel pin. He looks at David and offers his condolences for the loss of Silas, his father. David only winces. The Barghest grabs a box of cigars and a pickle to purchase. Behind his glasses, his pupils grow large and curious. "You gentlemen look glum. Perhaps a night at my establishment would help lift your spirits. The girly show would be on the house. Anything extra would be…extra." The Barghest presses his hand to his lapel pin and fidgets with it a fair bit. His teeth shine big.

"I'm a faithful man," says Marion, looking down at the ring over his swollen knuckle. These short years have been kind to him. Marion's been married twice now. His first wife died of a long illness very early in their marriage. And his second was because of a promise he'd made to himself. He almost was married another time, when his sister's friend was in trouble and the daddy left her. He almost married her but he was still grieving his first wife. The girl ended up trying to drown herself and was in that scary hospital in the city for life. The one where Danuel's son ended up. The baby didn't make it. Marion knew he would one day be called to help another little girl in trouble.

He loved the wife of his youth and loves the wife of his latter days wholly but in different wholes. He watches his son play hopscotch in the August sun.

"I know what kind of monster you are," says David.

The Barghest laughs so coldly that Marion adds, "It sours a soul." He places a five on the counter.

"Well, Mr. Chapman, there's the problem. I ain't got a soul to sour. Keep the extra moneys. I got plenty."

Before he leaves, he looks at the ceiling above, creaking where Marion's wife is upstairs nursing their new baby. He licks his lips. "Don't let her come my way, Mr. Chapman. You may be faithful. But I don't know about her."

When he's gone David says: "Can't stand the Barghest. Don't understand why everyone still goes to him. Belladonna's place is still open. You can't compete with that sort of show. Even if you had a radio."

"Hush up, man!"

They laugh.

UNTITLED

Nell is gathering bundles of sticks along the woods that skirt her house. Her husband, August, at work and her children at Miss Matilda's school, she enters into the meditation of home-making, a trance she places herself in daily. She peels back the layers of her mind and removes herself from herself. She learned the practice from Tata Duende, who used to travel with the circus, and he got it from a mesmerizer, who he said was a Turk of some kind. She chants and takes a little coughing powder. All the roars and whispers of the world cease. Nell is pure. Nell reaches into the sleepiness of the moment and can see herself from above, gathering the sticks.

She tugs her gaze away from her own eyes, seeing them not as brown dots in the mirror but as clear glass orbs through which she can see further into her body. She has been practicing this trance for months now, practicing piercing her vein with this miasma, practicing melting into her mind unseen, as Tata Duende says. The metathought almost brings her back to awake, but then she allows the waves of listless energy to creep their way up to the final zenith, monstrous waves cresting on an oxbow lake. There is the soul-locked mindset: she sees the sticks her body gathers, sees her own face, and sees the entire Bramble Patch at once and yet not completely.

Her name, being called from a little down the lane, awakes

her and draws her body back into her mind like the projector sucking the film back into itself.

"Nell..." It is a lingering singsong on the horizon, but a sweet one that leaves her without fear. She opens her eyes truly for the first time in so long, and the woods are umber with late autumn. Her mind is settled into the smallest pockets she can manage. And all through the woods before her, she smells traces of smoke and rain. She is one thing and another at this time and all others.

"Nell!" It's her husband. Running up to the house. Smiling. Paper in his hands.

"Jesus, August! You scare me a bit too well."

Her mind is still meditating in pulses of light, almost all sharp again, though. Her husband's gap, where his incisor is missing, threatens to suck her in as he barrels into her with a kiss. "Nell, guess what I got in my hand?" He shakes the paper in front of her unfocused eyes.

"Just a paper."

"Just a—just a paper? What you think, mm? You think I'm coming home midday for a piece of paper if it's not the most important piece of paper in our lives?"

Nell kisses him on the cheek. She can't read it, but she can feel joy vibrate from his skin into her bones. The osteons of her bones are filling with anticipation.

"Mr. Duncan says he going to ask me to do deliveries for him now and he just co-signed a loan for a truck. For us. We got—" He brings his voice down to the volume only ants, bees, and Nell can hear. "We got a Ford, Nell."

More quickly than she notices, Nell is in his arms, gracing him with kiss after kiss. Giant, timber-twisting laughter escapes out of her mouth, nose, ears, and eyes. Giant as thunder on the oxbow lake. Her mind snaps into focus, if for only a moment, like she's been popped in the mouth. Her whole body is smacked too. She doesn't let August see, though.

"I'm going to Marion's real quick to buy us some sugar so you can make the cinnamon cake, girl."

"Shit, August."

"And could you make your smothered cabbage?"

"What about our mule?"

"What about her?"

"What are we going to do with her with a truck now?"

"Truck's better than a mule."

"The roads turn to mud soon as someone sweats. Tillie ain't a truck, but she won't get stuck in the mud."

August kisses her with chapped lips, and she's a little too aware of how poor the two of them are. "Ha! Nell, you always worry, mm, about every little thing 'fore it needs worrying." He takes off down the road.

Nell knows that August won't bring back sugar. He'll bring liquor from Tempess's juke joint 'cross the river. She sighs and tries to return to the unearthly plane but instead settles into the ache near her heart where the excitement of the truck rests.

THESE BONES

Odessa was raisin brown when she born and grew darker sewing at Ma Lyons's side. She was stained with blackberry juice, ash, and bruises. And since her brother had died, she worked three times as hard at sewing. She watched Bit read in the corner and jealousy twisted her mouth. How could anyone have wanted to give her a benefactor after all that had happened? It made Odessa's nose start to rot from the inside out. Four years Marion and Bessie raised her nephew without knowledge of his daddy, and this daughter of a whore, she got to read the day away in a corner.

Odessa fingered the silk and lace bodice in her hands. She imagined her future husband coming to her own wedding, smelling like smoked meat and beer. "Ma, we're making a dress for that white girl's wedding. You think she would make my dress if we gave her enough money?"

Ma Lyons inspected the bodice work from over Odessa's shoulder. "You got a lot of nerve for someone who is taking her money. I like the beading work you did."

There was an ugly ball of strings that Odessa had to pull, each holding a weight at the end. She tugged each string, attempting to unravel her world. That she was taking money from the man who murdered her brother, from the family who hired her sister, that she would take the money and hide deeply into the woods with the chipmunks and bury it until it grew into a money tree. She went stargazing at night when she buried her money. She was in love with Orion, clung to his belt with a fist made of ice and until her hand melted into the dawn. He'd leave her during moonset; she would tug on the string and unravel the world. Under him, she was bold and bright like doll's daisies along the riparian field.

Odessa heard her sister come in heavy. She heard the heaviness in her voice and feet as she threw her arms around Ma. Esther's heaviness pressed them all to the corners of the room. Ma had already confessed to Odessa that she wished Esther would marry and leave.

"Missus Eugenia don't want me to come back after the wedding." Her voice was tears.

Ma could have said a story to make her feel better like she had when everyone was little. But instead she asked why.

"Mr. JJ and Croswell's leaving for school. And Penelope's gonna be married now. And she don't think she need me."

Well of course not, said Odessa. She had worked for them for near fifteen years now. All the kids were grown now. JJ and Croswell on their way to college in a few weeks. Penelope was marrying the man who murdered their brother. And Samuel kept placing his ink-stained hands on her hips, leaving bits of himself on Esther's dress.

Ma said it soured a soul. Levees broke in Esther. Levees break, Ma said. No, no, no, said Esther. And even Bit looked up from her book to listen to Esther. "They don't know."

Odessa watched Ma go to the stove to make some coffee.

THESE BONES

It was her way of letting Odessa know she could not handle Esther no more. Esther for her part began to shrink into the fabric of her dress until it grew larger than her.

"I know it's hard, Esther. You'll find another job. Or maybe it's time think about marrying. Maybe go stay with Aunt Phyllis for a while. She knows some men."

Esther looked at Bit in the corner. "What you reading?"

Bit lifted her chin from her chest. "Miss Boot assigned me some Shakespeare."

Esther laughed the way a hummingbird flies. "Full fathom five thy father lies. Of his bones are coral made."

Odessa tried to suss out what that would mean. But Esther leaned her head against Bit's shoulder and started to drift into her words. Odessa grabbed a swatch of river-blue silk and converted it to ribbons.

THE ISLE IS FULL OF NOISES
1930

It was raining. In the pattern of a tommy gun, of a war drum, of all the ghosts and bones Tempess knew were hiding in the river. She looked at her lover, Miss Phoebe. Then she looked at her daughter, Selene, her Moon-child.

"Rains come and go," Tempess heard the voice of her grandmother say. Another body under the water. Another ghost in her juke joint. She turned to her cousin, Rhea, and

Tata Duende. He held his little girl Snow-baby up to his chest, cradling her gently, whispering to her.

Rhea nodded to her child. "Daddy's right, honey girl!" She'd learned to etch out Kriol from the years of picking at it, the way a child picks at cold radishes on the dinner plate. Tata Duende's words were thick with Belizean vegetation, vines and branches curling through the gaps between his molars.

Tempess furrowed her brow. "Put Snow-baby down, Tata," she said. "Don't scare her."

The river began to knock at their door.

It was raining. At the edge of the Bramble Patch, folks were gathering sandbags and hay bales, hoping the rains would come then go.

"Sours a soul," said old Danuel as he looked at the river grown pregnant with ill omens. He sprinted down Mercer Street the only way an old man can. His body and spirit got soggy as he tried to make it home.

Staring at the empty stage of his girlie show, the Barghest was in a bowler hat and a velvet suit, listening to the water as she grew more impatient. He heard a creak from upstairs and jumped. No, it couldn't be. No one else was here today. Not with the waters rising and not when he had such an important customer coming. The drumming of rain grew louder.

It took Tempess a moment to realize that everybody was staring her down.

"Girl, did you hear me?" asked Rhea. Truth be no one could really hear as the rain galloped across the tin roof. Tempess shook her head. "Tell Snow-baby what the Bramble folk used to say about us when we were little."

Tempess's eyes darted to her little cousin. She was trembling in her father's arms, though she was bigger than him these days. Tempess forced a little laugh out of her lungs. "Them folks across the river used to say we were marsh-willow black. Wild black. The kind of black you can't ever touch."

Snow-baby's eyes just grew bigger.

Tempess said, "I don't like the way the river looks."

The river, she did look angry.

"Phoebe and I are going to shutter the place 'fore it comes. You know where the boat's moored. Get Moon-child up to the Bramble, would you?"

Selene turned briskly to face her mother.

"Tempess," Phoebe said, "it's just a storm."

But Tempess bit her lip and just said, "Rhea?" Like chopping the waves upon the prow.

Bertha's kin knew the water. The mind can say it's just a storm, but the blood knows it ain't true.

"Tata," Rhea said, "get the dinghy."

Tempess grabbed Selene's arm as she walked towards the door. "Moon-child, you Bertha's folk, you know the water; you don't need nothing but your body." She hugged her child and went back up to the juke joint. And that was all.

* * *

Nothing scared the Barghest, nothing started his heart. He was near eighty years old and had shed his own skin so often that he was barely anchored to his mortal body anymore. No, only the type of folks who were attached could be scared. That wasn't him. Still, the creak upstairs left him breathless. He was alone. He knew. He had checked. His mind landed on the pain rolling through his stomach. The creak came again. Then the knock at the door.

"You're drenched," said the Barghest as he opened the door.

Reverend Kincaid spat out rainwater onto the whiskey-warped floors. His galoshes spattered the weather across the Barghest's feet. His lips and nailbeds were nearly blue with cold.

"It's been a while, huh?" said the Barghest as he offered a seat to the Reverend.

"Aren't you tired of hearing you own voice yet?" snapped the Reverend. His throat began to close as angry tears neared the rims of his eyes.

"I'm not the one who's got a program on the radio. I'm just a part in your story, Reverend. I just…wanted you to have everything you ever wanted. Is that really so bad?"

The Reverend looked up. "I didn't want it."

The Barghest laughed. "Yes, you did. Every bit of it. Especially her. You woulda killed for that one. And you got it on the cheap. Me? I'm just a salesman, Reverend, same as you. You sell heaven, and I sell what people really want. And you

got life out of it. Ol' Bertha used to say, 'life gotta repay life.'
Did you know *her?*"

"Can't say I know many Negroes in town."

"Only the *one*, right?"

Steel could meet a jugular, you know. Reverend to pimp,
the need for blood swelled as the waters rose. A quick blade
could flay open the blood vessels; there could be whiskey and
rain and hemoglobin soaking the floors. But there was no fight
left in the Reverend. Only arteries hardened by dogma and
pride. The Barghest smacked his lips as saliva filled his mouth.
This feast was richer still than all the white and black bones
he could ever have eaten. He enjoyed the taste of skin and
decadent fat and loved to suck the marrow dry. But a man's
battered soul was sweeter yet.

There were sunflowers along the bank that sloped down to
the pebble-freckled shore at Tempess's place. Everyone would
forget that part, but in high summer, the sunflowers reached
up to heaven and praised the sky. And now the rain and wind
flattened them into mud. "They're meant to hold back the
world," Bertha had said. "Whatever white men and Bramble
folk think of us, the sunflowers will be a hedge of protection."
They stopped working when the Lyons boy's body washed
ashore. Now they were gone.

Rhea stripped down to nothing, her rich dark body bare,
and soon Moon-child, creamy and new, was also naked.
Tata and Snow-baby kept their clothes. Once the oxbow lake

pooled, it was only a matter of time before she, the river, took them over.

Tata climbed into the dinghy, his legs nearly busting through the rotted wood. "Wish we had built a new one before the waters came," Rhea said.

"We always promised that we would," said Selene.

Rhea clutched Snow-baby in one hand. "You gotta help your momma kick most of the way, okay?"

Moon-child went to the prow and drug the boat into the water. She turned moss green and shivering in the water up to her waist. Suddenly everything shifted, the oxbow lake pooled up and overflowed. The river came running.

She opened up like a split-lipped corn snake swallowing a dead rat, sending Rhea further down into the utmost chasms of water.

She kicked back and kicked back against death, holding her child, her little Snow-baby, feeling the wiggling heart-thumps within her chest. She could not hold on. Snow-baby slid away and into the water below. Rhea braced her daughter into her knee and then with the little strength she had into the dinghy with her father as it slumped into the river. The water was ashy gray and sick. Poisonous and kicking back. Snow-baby clawed into Tata and screamed over the roar of the current. Moon-child clung to the prow and flipped in the current. Rhea's fingers dug into the rotting wood of the stern; the lumber caved under the weight of her hands. The boat bucked and then reared up. The boat flipped. Down went

Tata and Snow-baby into the fathoms. Selene's body smacked waves. The waters crashed into Rhea's ears.

The fact was, as far as the Reverend could tell, the Barghest was right. He had gotten everything he had ever wanted. His daughter was married to the man she wanted. Samuel was long gone. That Black witch was out of his home and on her way to the institution. The little girl with his smile was out of town and no one had known her truth. And best of all, he'd had so many nights under wool blankets in an upstairs room with the redbone woman named Jess. The memory of her soft hands resting upon his chest, and the way her voice never wavered from a quiet hum, and how sometimes she curiously balked at his touch as if she understood that this was a beautiful game they played: he kept all of these moments in a dark corner. They were delicate, like stained glass in the church window; he had shored up all of it with lead and gold, and all the while he kept the faint hint of jasmine perfume in his memory. And as he handed over the money for the last time, a faint smile drifted on his lips.

The creak upstairs came again, and the Reverend jumped. "I thought you said we were alone."

The Barghest laughed. "All of us got ghosts, Reverend. Even me."

All these years of Bramble folk thinking this white man could hurt them. But the Barghest was an old bulldog with teeth to a point, and he knew how and where and when to bite. The Reverend wasn't the first white man to pay the Barghest. Hell, he wasn't even the only Kincaid who had. Nothing about the Reverend was all that special, the Barghest noted. He also smiled. This was it. All of the years of sulfur and soot and sex and sweat, and finally he could eat as much as he wanted anywhere he liked.

The two smiled as if they were friends. The Reverend shook hands with the pimp for what he hoped was the last time. Neither of them knew that the river had given birth, and the sandbags and hay bales were failing.

Selene later told her husband that "the water swallowed the world." And the river did take what she had; some things are inevitable. Phoebe and Tempess disappeared beneath the waves. The river took Snow-baby down to the riverbed. The river takes nothing but what was hers first.

By the time Rhea found air again, she couldn't see the boat or her family. But her tired eyes saw the land, and she made it up to the edge of the river, knowing the water was coming up higher and higher. She got up and ran naked to a swath of higher ground in the Bramble Patch.

The white man there was as familiar to her as any could be. He was weathered, drenched in rain and doubt, bow-legged and heavy in his eyes. Fire was in his feet. His shadow lengthened without the sun.

Rhea caved into a house of flora, a bush beaten with rain,

and watched him leave the back alley of the Barghest's place. She was naked and ashamed in his presence.

But then something happened when the other two whites appeared. She knew the man and the woman, too. He was the monster of Napoleonville who had bloodied the Lyons boy, and she, his new bride and daughter of the Reverend. She could make out their faces even as the water rose; she felt it creeping up her heels and wanting to drag her down into the river.

The Reverend looked up to see his Penny and her husband sloshing through the mud towards him. He held his hands outstretched towards them. The sting of her slap that followed startled him. He stumbled to the mud. As he stood up to return the blow, his towering son-in-law stood between them.

"What in God's name is wrong with you, girl!" he roared.

"Reverend Kincaid. Frequent fornicator and Negro-loving son of a bitch!" she yelled. Her eyes glowed with hatred.

"You will not speak to me like that. I'm still your father, young lady!"

"Shut up, old man!" Penny raised her hands to her hair and tugged tight. "You couldn't even keep your suspenders on while half the town's looking for you. You nearly killed my brother over these whores!"

"I'm not here for that! I have business."

"In Mercy City?" asked Penny.

The Reverend's heart stopped at the primal growl in his daughter's voice. The rain beat down on the remnants of his memories in this spot, behind the Barghest's place. He thought of when the stars dimmed overhead and he looked up into Jessup's window and saw her slip into a robe and then turn off her kerosene lamp. How he would walk home and practice his Sunday sermon over and over on the way up the hill to the white side of Napoleonville. How feverishly delicious it all was. And in this moment, as the world began to flood, the memories brought the hint of a smile to his face. As his smile faded, a blackness filled his daughter's eyes.

For a breath or two, Rhea did not look at the three white folks arguing. She watched the water, hoping it wouldn't reach her before these white folks left, hoping her family would appear from the waves, hoping the river would spare some part of the past. And she kept looking at the water until she heard what sounded like a fish being gutted barbels to caudal.

Then she looked and saw the eruption of blood coming from the Reverend's throat. He became marinated in his own blood and fell as a paper doll into the ground. She screamed and stood up from the pricker bush as he bled out.

Penelope's eyes caught Rhea's, and they carried hate in them. Their eyes met together with a hateful caress like lovers meeting in secret.

Rhea tore off into the trees where the waters were rising. Naked. Terrified. Until she found something that resembled safety in the woods.

THESE BONES

When the waters overtook the shore, there was a great cry in the Bramble Patch. The lingua franca of a people who could not conceive of the world changing. Yet the waters did not stop, no matter that they put the sandbags up against what was once the shore. Up and down Mercy City, the shadow of death, her riparian steed, the easterly winds, diagonal telegram lines, pockets of dust, pavement, urbane lipstains, beer, the skeletal remains of Bessie's other son, all this flooded the rows of iniquity. The whole world drowned, but Reverend Kincaid was not upon it.

It felt like a whole eternity before Rhea was sitting in Marion Chapman's store, in the embrace of her husband and baby cousin. They wept until they had wrung the water from themselves inside and out. Then they left town, because the river had taken everything but their lives and the white woman would take those, too, if she could tell one darkie from another.

When many years had passed Selene would sit with her husband and her ancient cousin, Rhea, in a little house in Napoleonville. Selene's husband would weep at the dinner table as the truth came to him.

"Few things I know for sure," said Rhea. "Your sister and her husband killed your father, the Reverend Kincaid; I saw it as you see me now. They'll dredge up the river, honey, and they'll churn up the blood-red mud and soon they will find all the tiny bones folks thought they were careful to hide. Your father will be there, and Selene's mama, and my Snow-baby. And the last thing I know for sure, there will come a day when all of it will be memory. The river will erode the memories of the land. But us? The people? We will always be here."

THE BRAMBLE CLEARED

In 1965, the last roof in the Bramble Patch caved in, crushing Nell underneath rotting wood and the weight of her own heroin-eaten temporal lobe. Her children had long since left her, her husband had long since OD'd. She was in her eighties, old enough to want death. So as the beams creaked, she laid in her bed and closed her eyes. Her husband's Ford truck was what she saw as the roof fell upon her.

Up at the top of the hill, Peter and his wife, Penelope, watched from their car as the last house of the Bramble Patch fell. A Black boy ran between them and the Bramble Patch. Peter could not see the boy; his cataracts made the world misty. His wife held a flask to his lips, and he pushed it away. "Sistie, don't."

"It's bourbon. You like bourbon."

"The houses are gone."

Her liver-spot-speckled hand squeezed his cheeks. His tongue lolled from his flaccid lips and he slit the dorsal surface against his incisors. His dentures were made of sharpened ivory, adorned in steel.

"Did you want coffee, Peter? Cause we don't have a thermos," Penelope said. He shook his head. "Bourbon will make it easier."

"Zehowzezehgone," he stuttered.

"I heard you the first time."

Peter smacked away her hand. She let go of his cheeks. "You don't understand, Sistie. The houses are gone. The *people* are not."

Penelope caught her own eyes in the rearview mirror. The city of Napoleonville was behind them, shopping on a Sunday. Her father's picty came to mind. She hated sinners but hated her father more. Somewhere just in the corner of her—

"Peter, what's the pink part of the eye called? In the corner there?"

"It's called the lacrimal caruncle."

—the corner of her lacrimal caruncle, in the space where she was aware she had a nose but her brain had eliminated it from her field of vision, she felt the darkie called Esther standing there. Esther was in the cobwebbed corners of Penelope's mind; Esther felt Penelope from far, far away.

"Shut up, Peter!"

She grabbed his cheeks and forced his tongue out of his mouth. She grabbed her brother Samuel's knife from Peter's bag. "Like a paring knife against a pear," Peter had told her. She dug the knife into the flesh. Blood fountained from his mouth until there was no tongue, only a hunk of pink in her hand.

She got out of the car with tongue in one hand and a trowel in the other. She sort of missed the dirt road days but found a little place in the ditch where the overpass was. Cars thundered above her; she watched as her husband tried to plug the wound in his mouth with cotton balls. Next to a patch of wild Queen Anne's Lace—or hemlock, she didn't care if it was either anymore—she clawed the trowel and then her fingers into the dirt. She placed her husband's tongue inside the hole. She left it there under the highway, just before the hedges.

She got back into the car. The leather on the dash was covered with dark, dark blood. Peter looked ashen, but the bleeding had stopped. His cheekbones were collecting his tears.

"It's done, okay? It's done. I buried it so that not even God could hear it."

He shook his head gently.

"Don't you understand? The whole place's gone now. The whole place…if you could have held your tongue, Peter. If you could have just fucking held your tongue. Damn it. No one's going to know. You understand?"

She did not notice his shaking. She didn't notice how the shaking grabbed his whole body and mind. And even if she did, she didn't want to take him to the hospital. Not today. "Who even cares anymore? The houses are gone. The Bramble Patch is gone."

THESE BONES

Peter's last thought before the seizure drove him into unconsciousness was, "But the people are still here."

FROM "THE REMAKING OF AN AMERICAN CHURCH" (WOMAN'S HOME COMPANION, MARCH 1949)

By Daniel Butcher

This Middle American church has been transformed under the leadership of Reverend Jacob Jonah "JJ" Kincaid, the grandson of the church's founder, Reverend Samuel Wilkerson Kincaid. Now this hundred-year-old congregation, one of the oldest in this area still operating, faces new challenges and changes at the dawn of the second half of our century.

In the summer of 1909, this little slice of earth called Napoleonville was a world unto itself, isolated from outside influences.

Reverend Jacob Jonah Kincaid's father, the Rev. Jonah Kincaid, was preaching from the very pulpit the son now uses. "My father was fire and brimstone, through and through. People in this town were scared of him. They're scared of me, too. Just not exactly in the same way."

The reverend was just a young boy, then aged seven, when his mother hired a local Negro woman to look after him and his siblings. Their companionship throughout his childhood changed his life.

"She was odd yet kind, a miracle wrapped in skin. I came to understand that life was unequal for her and her family as time went on. Really, I owe her everything."

JJ, as he is called, has turned his father's church into the first fully integrated church in his area.

Sunday arrives beautifully clear and warm. JJ introduces me and my photographer to the congregation. "I know we aren't used to journalists sticking cameras in our faces, but act natural. No one here is Gary Cooper." He asks the congregation to bow their heads in prayer, and then one of his parishioners sprints in, mid-prayer. JJ laughs. "Father, forgive Brother Miller this morning. Just because he is in Your family, and we all know family is everything, doesn't mean he can come in when he feels like." Everyone suppresses a laugh together. "Amen!" they say in one voice.

The choir, which includes JJ's daughter Beatrice and the tardy Brother Miller, rushes to the front of the church to lead the congregation in song: first, "How Firm a Foundation," next, "Rock of Ages," and finally a livelier one called "Love Is My Wonderful Song."

In essence, the whole endeavor seems as typical as any Sunday in Anytown, America. But the faces in the congregation are anything but typical.

Today, the reverend preaches on the Psalms, the lyrics of King David. Specifically the 95th Psalm: "For the Lord is a great God, and a great King above all gods. In his hand are the deep places of the earth: the strength of the hills is his also. The sea is his, and he made it: and his hands formed the dry land." A smattering of "Amen!" and "Hallelujah!" erupts from the church. Later, Negro congregant Dinah Lyons will remark, "That verse has a different meaning here than it would anywhere else in the world." I suppose I am not in on the joke.

The Napoleonville Second Baptist was originally founded in the 1850s by Reverend Kincaid's grand-father, Samuel Wilkerson Kincaid I. It was once the largest congregation in the white district of this town. When JJ left home for college, he had no intention of shepherding his father's flock. "My brother Sam was groomed from childhood to take over when our father retired, and frankly, I wanted to get out of here as soon as I could. Then Mother got ill while I was at divinity school. Then my father was killed in the big flood of 1931. Samuel couldn't pastor the church anymore, so I took over."

His wife, Mrs. Selene Kincaid, says: "This building used to be the most crowded place in town on a Sunday. But when JJ took over and opened the doors to everyone, most people left. Then again, new people showed up as well."

People such as Sally and Geraldine "Deenie" Ailey, sisters—both lifelong residents of this area. "Our father Peter was a friend of the Kincaid family, especially Reverend Jacob's older brother and sister," says Sally. "My sister and I left the church for a while when Reverend Jonah started his radio program. He was crazy in those days. Then my father and his wife started staying away, when they found out that JJ would be taking over instead of Samuel. Especially because of their views on Negroes."

"We were wrong," says the elder sister, Geraldine. "About…many things. We started coming here a couple months ago, I think. It was strange at first, because we sit next to a Negro woman, but now she and Sally talk about baseball and swap recipes."

After service, the Reverend and I sit down at a local diner. "Good afternoon, Magnolia," JJ says. The waitress eyes him a moment and then pours him a glass of water. He exchanges smiles with her, introduces me, and orders me a cup of much needed coffee. With my coffee comes more bemused expressions throughout the diner.

After he orders lunch—a fried ham and egg sandwich and a side of cottage cheese—he takes out a travel brochure from his sport coat and reads it like a menu. "Lookithere! Selene and I are planning our first vacation since Bea [their daughter] was little. California and Mexico. Just us two. I can't stop thinking about it. Bea's going to stay with Selene's family while we're gone. She just turned fourteen, or fifteen. Never can remember. But it's all day on the phone with her friends or trying to go to the YMCA pool in Marion. My wife's a bit younger than I am, so she gets it more than I do. But Selene also grew up in these parts. Before we had paved roads, when it was still very segregated. She gets me, too. She's the bridge between Bea and me."

As we wait for our plates, I start asking a bunch of questions spitfire.

"Why the beard?"

"People think I'm crazy anyway, so I decided to look the part. I take after those old-time mountain preachers from the pioneer times. Plus, I look so much like my father these days, I have to distinguish myself."

"Favorite verse in the Bible?"

"You're only asking that because I'm a reverend."

"Fine, favorite book?"

"*Gulliver's Travels* and then *Connecticut Yankee* and then the Bible and then *Elmer Gantry*."

"That last one surprises me."

"It shouldn't. Man like me can learn a lot from it."

"Were you putting on a nice act for me, when really you're more fire and brimstone, or...? "

"Ha. You caught me on a fiery day. No, I find the Words of God in the whispers of the river. You want fire? That was my father all the way. He saw Hell and damnation everywhere he looked. Even in our home. Sometimes I wonder if he was preaching to himself mostly. No man is perfect. Least of all us in the pulpit."

"Favorite meal?"

"I guess I have two. Esther would make this pork and apple pie on my birthday. It was my favorite thing in the world. My wife's folks, they were originally from the Carolinas. Did you ever have fried green tomatoes? I didn't until we met and married. I'd been missing so much."

"What do you do to relax?"

"Go fishing. Listen to the radio. I like Tommy Dorsey. I sometimes bake. Esther taught me how. Selene is pretty good but my jumbleberry pie has hers beat."

"You mentioned your brother is a minister as well?"

"Samuel was supposed to be. He got tangled in other things, though. It sours a soul."

I ask JJ what the phrase means. He chuckles. "It's just something folks say around here."

"What makes that fact 'sour' your soul?"

"It wasn't that ministry wasn't for Samuel. More he wasn't for it, I think. He knew the Good Book backwards and forwards, but he'd be happier as a... scholar, maybe? Our little brother, Croswell, is an architect. He never even dreamed of taking up the family business."

"You seem quite normal. I thought you'd be more fanatical."

"Thank you. I feel quite normal myself."

"So I have to ask the Big Question: Why are you so insistent on integrating your church?"

"What a question! Ha! Let me ask you a question: Why are you a writer?"

He didn't wait for my reply.

"What's flesh and bone and ash—this matter we are—is just stuff. And at the end of all things, it'll be pulverized. So we mustn't pretend as if the differences between us are anything but fleeting atoms, bound for decay. We think the world has lines of demarcation, between us and them, the whole and the broken, the dark and the light, the living and the dead. But those lines aren't really there. In reality, what is the difference between the sea and the wave? After Bea was born and with the War, restlessness overtook me, and I saw in the haze of summer glimpses of what Esther told me. I couldn't help but wonder if there was anything for me to do but follow the path laid out."

Suddenly, he seemed distant, pensive, and indeed a little crazy.

"What path is that?" I asked.

"To put into motion these mechanisms of finality."

"I don't understand."

"Neither did I. And Esther, she's long gone from here, so she can't properly explain it to me. She was stolen into the night air when those who loved her weren't looking. But she has one last task in the fate of this town left. And then, to quote my favorite Bible verse, 'It is finished.'"

THESE BONES

"Who was this Esther?"

"In practical terms, she was the Negro my mother hired to help take care of my brothers, sister, and me."

"Is that all?"

"Of course not! But beyond that, I couldn't tell you. Enigmatic? That's a big silver-dollar word. Enigmatic Esther. My sister used to tell me she was a witch. But my sister's a little crazy. Think it's a family trait."

"And you attribute your current feelings on the matter of integration to your family's nursemaid?"

"I'm not so ungrateful as to use that terminology. I was a strange and shy child who wanted to be righteous and pretended to be cruel, because cruelty was a trait among righteous people here. I'd like to think I'd have come to the conclusion of integration myself after years of study and reflection, but I know I wouldn't have. I'd have gone on thinking my cruel thoughts and never seeing beyond them. I'm no one, really, but a boy who was forced to observe the world. It took eyes that could see beyond the waves to make out the sea. And I don't think I was even Esther's favorite of us."

When our food comes, JJ is mostly silent. Occasionally, he will offer a fact about local flora and fauna, especially about the fishing in the area—he is fond of flathead catfish—and where to listen to great music. As he finishes the cottage cheese, he stares at me for a moment and tells me how his mother and father's families were among the earliest settlers of this town.

"This church has been in the family for over a hundred years now, and I'm only its third pastor. That's a legacy. My mother's family, the Croswells, were really, really wealthy for most of the last century. Big spender types. That's a legacy, too. And my legacy will be the end of theirs."

I ask him what he means by that and he laughs. He is charming, certainly, and for all his insanity, he has a heart that truly believes.

"Two things may clear up what I mean," he says. "First, when I look at Selene and Bea, I feel relief. The Kincaid last name's going to die in these parts. Croswell's never coming back. My sister's married and they don't have… well, she doesn't even speak to me, 'cause her husband thinks I robbed Samuel of this place. And Samuel's no more fit for fatherhood than he is for the pulpit. I'll be the last Kincaid in this church and this town. I embrace that, find it comforting even."

Mrs. Kincaid walks into the diner, still wearing her tartan dress and bakelite necklace. Even Magnolia's hard face softens at the sight of the reverend's wife. She apologizes for the intrusion and reminds her husband that he is obliged to attend a family evening with his daughter, his wife, and her family. He shrugs at me and kisses her hand.

"What about that second thing?" I ask as the reverend stands up to go.

"There is more to us than what we see. Each of us is bones and spirit, water and fire, Sunday holiness and Saturday hully-gully. Each of us is our past and our present and our future, collapsed into one being. And we are all made of the dust we call home. Even if this is the end and they bury our bones, that's fine. Because where the bones lay buried, the spirit can still dance. And when the spirit still dances, well, brother, these bones will rise again."

'DEED I KNOW IT, SISTER

Jesus curse a fig tree, I curse a bramble bush. I curse the first and last of us, from 'Livia Marvell to Nell, I curse us. I curse us no more than we already been cursed. Cursed are these holy orphans who sprung fully formed from the mouth of the Sandstone River but blessed are their children who will not inherit the Bramble Patch, the river, Napoleonville, Lazarus's stuffed remains, Tempess's bloated drowned body, my lobotomized mind split into half-spheres with an icepick while I looked my brother's murderer in the eye. The icepick tore the curtain, tore away the feeble little bits of Esther Lyons, crazy witch of the Bramble Patch. They all thought the tar babies would go away when they turned my brain into two but they were tar babies all along, too. When you split an atom, the world explodes, so too when you split the brain, Dr. Peter. But now he laid up in this hospital, too, tongue gone and mind as well, locked up where he locked us. Now there isn't a ward for one or the other type of person, but all persons. He will die of Negro diseases and I will die of white ones.

Bessie stood in the river's cold. She stood ten paces or so away from her baby's grave. He was breech blue at birth and death, a moment enfolded as one, but expanded to an eternity of possibilities. Bessie was the river's cold before she knew it, dangling her own chattering teeth from her mouth. But she liked it that way. Lazarus told her once that a river winds through hell, her delta at the mouth, and twists and bends and thrusts into the cave walls of hell. Here the fire and water cannot kill each other; here they are not quenched. And where Lyman's twin lies, ten paces from the river in a hole covered by a gray, gray, gray rock, there was also hell. She was river-cold and probably river-mad, too. Marion was sweeping the store, Lyman was playing hopscotch with Snow-baby, Luella was asleep in the crib, milkdrunk. Bessie was the cold. She beat her hands against the stones and felt nothing. Bessie was eroding the Bramble Patch and turning fire and water into hell. Bessie was drowning. "I could wash away the entire Bramble Patch. Dig it up from root to root to root." She held the bones of her baby to her chest. Bessie drug her body onto the shore, where her lungs were filled with air and she was made of flesh and not water. Nothing drowned her here. But had she dared look into the water, she'd have seen her cursed self in the river, a river-mad reflection. She cursed us, and we cursed her back and the river, too.

That baby, he was one of the tar babies, too, and Laz and Jessup and 'Livia, and all the way back to the first one, her belly busted in pregnant meditation, singing dese bones g'wine rise again.

Selah! In holy meditation, I could see them all and everything they touched turned tar, too, and withered at the vine. The girl—no more a woman than I was, and more of a child, even—she was first death the Barghest caused, his own crude matter who was called mother but never got to hold her child. She died as he cannibalized her and then the whole Bramble Patch. I know it! 'Deed I know it, Sister. I know it! Dese bones g'wine rise again.

I am Black. Comely. Golden fleece woven. Started from behind. Brain split in two. That part's not new, I was always half here and half in the future, looking at Danuel's son drooling out in the future and in my present at the dinner table, unable to lift a fork to his mouth. I got my faculties. When Mister Croswell was a young'un, he and I talk this talk:

"How come Samuel can go to the Bramble Patch?"

"Because he's a grownup, I suppose he can do what he wants to."

"But you're older than Samuel and you can't do what you want to."

"That's different."

"How come?"

"It has been made that way."

"What do you suppose he does over there?"

"He does bad things."

"What kind of things?"

"Things you don't have to worry about."

"What sort of things happen down there? ...You're taking too long."

"Give me a moment."

"Well?"

"Fragile things happen there."

Somehow, I got out into the darkness and out the hospital. "Folks say somehow they did something. But Somehow always means God," Ma Lyons used to say to me. Lord, lead my hemispheres into the dark places, where the pieces of cold, cold winter cannot shrivel me up. The tar babies follow me. We are going to Death's door.

He watched pebbles scatter before the wind. He watched fallow, flood, and famine. He watched men grow from boys in the curled tendrils of euphoria. He watched a habanera dance a thousand times. He was an observer of life rather than its own participant. And while 'Livia Marvell swore he sold his soul to the devil until she was so senile as to believe it to be true, the truth was he might not have had enough of a soul to sell in the first place. Where he went, only death followed, and with him, the tar babies came.

Down to the river, when they baptized Wanhope just before she left for school, a butterfly landed on the crown of her head. And she beat her wings against Wanhope's braids and laid her dust across each of the kinks in her hair. Wanhope had not gotten in the water yet, but she suddenly did not want to go in. She stood toe deep with the butterfly adorning her. Wanhope looked at me and I understood. She had been baptized already; "Somehow" had come and kissed her forehead with His anointing. The water would wash the butterfly dust from her soul, when she was already cleansed in His glory. She ran from the water, barefoot, like her mother walking along the river's edge to leave her. The way Jessup's ma'am danced upon the floorboards when she spoke the word *hope* into the dust. Bit ran into the dust of Hope and leapt towards the sagging house where the Barghest traded flesh. She knelt into the paved road, and her tears became a baptism of a sort as well. She would not be touched, from that day on. She would leave and be something other than a child of prickers and briars. She belonged to "Somehow."

Truth follows the lies. I sniff for the Barghest.

Everything they touch turns to tar. Even me over time. I am turning to tar, every day, slowly, and I stick to the walls, ash, and silk. I remember the skirts trailing the ground and I remember standing on Mercer Street telling everyone to repent. But now Babylon is dismantled; New Jerusalem is coming. Someone Negro is living in the old Keith house, someone Negro is living in the old Kincaid house, and someone Negro is living in the Ailey house. And when the last house came down on Nell's head, it was finished.

I am Black. Comely. Satisfied by eating at the same table as Danuel's son and Dr. Peter. Don't twist my words, though. Satisfied ain't happy. Satisfied ain't free. "Somehow" is watching over me. He's got me nestled in a huddle by His breast. He leads me to the apartment building in the city. I cling to the bus, and in the city, I am unknowable. I eat at a Kresge's counter, thinking of Marion's body hung up from the rafters of his store and Luella and Lyman crying but Bessie too struck by the thunder. It was the second time a man she had children with died with a noose around his neck. She had grown numb to it all. The lady who served my tomato soup spat in it and stirred it with her acrylic nail to hide her sin, but I taste her in every bite. I don't mind, because I am hungry and I need to be nourished.

I am Black. Comely. Followed by a brood of tar babies. They followed me all of my life, and that's why Dr. Peter and Penelope sent me to be locked up in his hospital. To be given insulin to set me into dreamless sleeps for days. To be electrocuted in searing hot mind storms until I was almost docile enough to be tortured again. But I never had a knack for listening. To watch my Bramble Patch neighbor, shellshocked still after the War, have his brain carved up like the Easter ham. To have them try the same on me. Penelope came for my lobotomy. She came to watch me, smiled and called me a bitch. I just laughed at her. Cause I knew what she had done, I knew why she watched the Bramble Patch every day, waiting to find the woman who saw her kill her father. But I never told her that Rhea and her folks are long, long gone. Except Selene. I never told Penelope that her sister-in-law was a mulatto either. It cut too deep to hear that; she'd have gone mad herself and killed Mister JJ and Selene and their daughter. Misters JJ and Croswell, they are fine for what they are. They had me, and the tar babies never touched them.

In *Foxe's Book of Martyrs* my name would not appear, because I tread lightly on this earth.

"Somehow" guides me to the apartment, which is old enough that the windows have cataracts. The brick crumbles, the mortar is keloided. Every inch of me now feels the stitches in my clothes wrap around my muscles. I have been around the sun enough times to recognize the taste in my mouth is my own bleeding gums. This is the road that don't lead back to alive.

His nurse is old, dressed in white; she spoons jello into his mouth. It turns his tongue red.

"You know I'm over a hundred. I been on this earth so long I remember when Lincoln ran it."

"Is that right?"

"I used to run a girly show. That was my trade. I traded in dances and sex."

The nurse blushes pink under brown. I am at the window, sitting at the balcony, peeking my eyes to see them; I cling to the wall. She turns on the television and adjusts the rabbit ears. In the dim blue glow, I can see the Barghest, a crinkled old man, sprouting hair and sagging jowls but still smug.

His hands grab the nurse's wrist. "You'd have been good on my stage. Sweet as you is." Her heart is humming, and his eyes catch hers. Then he lets her go and laughs. "Git!" The woman scurries out of the room. His dull eyes roll up towards his brows.

"No need to sit out in the cold," he says. "Come on in here."

I am looking into his face and he sees nothing. There are ballet dancers on the television; strains of melodies sing above the slight hum of the static incoming. Their backs are straight and narrow, flexing at the shoulder joint, locked in the moment.

Out of my bones comes the knelling of bells and the deferred dreams of all my little tar babies. I don't think I can kill him, but I don't have to. "You remember me?" I ask.

"Only by reputation."

"Good." I look at his drooping lips and place mine on his. They still taste of blood after years and years. "You are Death."

"And you Black. Comely. I don't need to tell you the obvious, so don't you do it to me. Shit, woman."

"Then you know why I'm here?"

He laughs like dusty bellows stoking the fire to life. "You can't kill me. You're a loony that they tossed away. Bramble Patch is gone. They all started moving up the hill. We're relics to them. You know what a relic is?"

"You tell me."

"It's something so damn old and dusty that it's got to be locked away."

"And holy."

"What?" he says. The growl in his voice returns.

"A relic is a holy thing, known to have power. You right about me, but you not right about you. They locked me away and vivisect my brain, and I'm still a holy thing." The tar babies grow restless, each of them ones he stole life from.

He says, "You ain't shit. You just a crazy."

No. He's not right. Because I picked peaches as a girl, then raised them white babies, then I was a crazy in the crazy house. But now, I'm a debt collector.

"'Deed I know, brother."

In a procession, they emerge from my shadow, the dozen or so ravaged souls. They melt and sag and weather under the years but grow and grow and grow till the blue light of the television is extinct. We are all perfumed in their rage.

When he was a boy, the one they call the Barghest stepped into the river and saw a man, who 'Livia Marvell swore was the devil. She saw them talk and shake hands. And no matter the misfortune that befell him from that day on, he always managed to stay alive. When the flood waters came, he lassoed the folk of the Bramble Patch together and fashioned a raft. When the fires would rage, he hung their bodies as an asbestos curtain. He did this until the Bramble Patch began to turn into a mirage. When he was a child, he walked into the river and stained his soul with ink and blood, cursed us all with him. But I curse back; I curse us all. Myself, too. The fig tree withered under Christ's words, and here the blackest berries in the Patch lift themselves out from the tangle of thorns.

They grab him, limbs in hand, tugging him apart. The one who was my brother reaches his hand through the Barghest's belly. Death screams and Lazarus pulls out the guts which are swole up. He is swaddled in tar. The one who was Jessup rakes her fingernails against his radial artery; he does not bleed but the pain is real. The one that was Ida rips tufts of cotton hair from his scalp. The others dance around him singing that spiritual: "Lawd thought he'd make 'im a man. Made 'im outta mud and a han'fula san'." Then the first one, belly full with pregnancy, looks her child in the eye and reaches her claw hands into his mouth and down his throat. His eyes get wide and wider still. She smiles like a mother at the sight of her child, reaches further down. He starts shaking, faster and worse until he's 'bout rattling. Suddenly his eyes burst white and he screams with no sound but the echo of horror. He collapses, slack, ragdoll-like. His mother's hand retreats from his mouth, where she holds his still-fluttering heart.

She throw it to the ground and it hits with a *sploosh*. She sticks out her tongue and laughs and laughs and laughs. Her body, tar body, is iridescent, or maybe it's the glow of the television behind her. She and I look each other in the face; we've known each other over fifty years, and I laugh, too. We little girls again. But I think I laugh too loud, because his nurse's voice catches my mind. All my tar babies, long as I carried them with me, are gone.

I run back to the balcony and leap into the darkness. And fall. And drown in nighttime. And there is no bottom to the fall. Nothing but black. I am baptized into the night and I know what the river hides. They will not find what they seek, only an old man whose heart stopped beating. The Bramble Patch, turned to star thistles.

The wind tumbles in the high grass and skips over the Sandstone River. I hit the pavement and all caves in—my skull included. "Somehow" is watching over me from above. And I watch him too. My eyes are festooned with stars. Holy water flows from my nose and ears. But 'deed, I know it, sister. Dese bones g'wine rise again.

ACKNOWLEDGMENTS

I would like to thank everyone who helped me create *These Bones*. From inception to publication, so many people have been there. It really takes a village to raise a novella. My undying gratitude first goes to the team at Lanternfish Press—Christine Neulieb, Feliza Casano, and Amanda Thomas—who have been absolutely phenomenal in guiding me through the process of publication.

Thank you to Professor Matt Kirkpatrick at Eastern Michigan University, who acted as the advisor for the project that eventually became *These Bones* and who, from the word "jump," had absolute faith in the project.

I'm thankful for my personal village, too. Thank you to my family—especially my parents, Cheryl and Jonathan Shumake and the late Richard Chenault—for your love of stories, your encouragement to forge my own path, and your excitement for me whenever I came to you with new ideas I had written, especially all the ones I wrote about dogs when I was seven. Of which there were many. To my friends, colleagues, and classmates who have constantly read my work and hyped me up, even if it meant being subjected to a thirty-minute lecture about the history of American music that you never asked for. Specifically, I would like to shout out Daniel Wiland and Bethany Metivier for acting as friend-editors and beta readers as I worked on *These Bones*.

Lastly, I would be remiss without acknowledging the works I read while working on *These Bones*. I have been very fortunate to read some amazing books that helped shape me. So, though they will never see this, thank you to Fran Ross, Alan Lomax, Toni Morrison, Anna-Marie McLemore, and Ishmael Reed for the words you put out into the universe.

ABOUT THE AUTHOR

KAYLA CHENAULT IS a practitioner of Black Girl Magic and holds a Master's in Creative Writing from Eastern Michigan University. When she is not writing, Kayla is found at the museums where she works or telling everybody about the history of popular music and social dance. She is a former line editor and contributing writer for *Cecile's Writers*. Her previous work can be found in *The Blue Pages Journal* and *Honey and Lime* literary magazine.